Elidor

A street-map, a deserted demolition site, a football and a church in ruins are the four ordinary things on an ordinary grey day in Manchester that lead Roland, Helen, Nicholas and David into *Elidor*, 'the Green Isle of the Shadow of the Stars,' but a twilight world almost destroyed by fear and darkness. Now only the four children can save *Elidor* from total desolation by guarding four treasures which preserve in them the possibility of *Elidor's* salvation. But gradually the powers of evil start to invade the quiet Manchester suburbs. Is it only static electricity that makes the television howl? Why do damp patches appear on the attic wall—or are they men's shadows? And why do the children feel the relentless pull of a deep and numbing terror?

'Each detail, ordinary or sinister, establishes atmosphere, background or character exactly. *Elidor* is a remarkable book; intelligent, rich and terrifying.'

Times Literary Supplement

The Moon of Gomrath, The Weirdstone of Brisingamen and *The Owl Service* are also in Lions.

Also by Alan Garner
in Lions

The Weirdstone of Brisingamen
The Moon of Gomrath
The Owl Service
Red Shift

ELIDOR

Alan Garner

Illustrated by Charles Keeping

COLLINS · LIONS

First published in 1965 by William Collins Sons & Co Ltd
14 St James's Place, London sw1
First published in Lions 1974
5th Impression 1976

Printed in Great Britain by
William Collins Sons & Co Ltd Glasgow

For J.H.

Contents

"Childe Rowland to the Dark Tower came——"

KING LEAR, *act iii, sc.* 4

1. Thursday's Child

'All right,' said Nicholas. 'You're fed up. So am I. But we're better off here than at home.'

'It wouldn't be as cold as this,' said David.

'That's what you say. Remember how it was last time we moved? Newspapers on the floor, and everyone sitting on packing cases. No thanks!'

'We're spent up,' said David. 'There isn't even enough for a cup of tea. So what are we going to do?'

'I don't know. Think of something.'

They sat on the bench behind the statue of Watt. The sculptor had given him a stern face, but the pigeons had made him look as though he was just very sick of Manchester.

'We could go and ride on the lifts in Lewis's again,' said Helen.

'I've had enough of that,' said Nicholas. 'And anyway, they were watching us: we'd be chucked off.'

'What about the escalators?'

'They're no fun in this crowd.'

'Then let's go home,' said David. 'Hey, Roland, have you finished driving that map?'

Roland stood a few yards away, turning the handles of a street map. It was a tall machine of squares and wheels and lighted panels.

'It's smashing,' he said. 'Come and look. See this roller? It's the street index: each one has its own letter and number. You can find any street in Manchester: it's easy. Watch.'

Roland spun a wheel at the side of the map, and the index whirled round, a blur under the glass.

'There must be some pretty smooth gears inside,' said Nicholas.

The blur began to flicker as the revolving drum lost speed. Roland pressed his finger on the glass.

'We'll find the one I'm pointing at when it stops,' he said.

The drum turned slowly, and the names ticked by: and the drum stopped.

' "Thursday Street",' said Helen. 'Mind your finger. "Ten, seven L".'

'Ten will be the postal district,' said Roland. 'You turn the map wheel until number seven is level with these squares painted red on the glass, and then Thursday Street is in square L. There.'

'I can't see it,' said Nicholas.

The map square was full of small roads, some too short to hold the name even when it was abbreviated. But at last the children found a 'Th. S.' jumbled among the letters.

'Titchy, isn't it?' said David.

'It's such a funny name,' said Roland: 'Thursday Street. Shall we go and see what it's like?'

'What?'

'It's not far. We're in Piccadilly, here, and Thursday Street's off to the right up Oldham Road. It shouldn't be hard to find.'

'I might have known you'd think of something daft,' said Nicholas.

'But let's do it,' said Helen. 'Please, Nick. You and David'll only start scrapping if we don't. And when we've found it we'll go home: then nobody's bossed about.'

'OK,' said David. 'That's all right by me.'

'It's still daft,' said Nicholas.

'Can you think of anything?'

'Oh, all right. This is your idea, Roland, so you take us. Can you find the way?'

'I think so. We'll go up Oldham Road for a bit, and then cut through the back streets.'

They left Watt. David and Nicholas were better tempered now that there was something positive to be done.

'This is the turning we want,' said Roland after a while. 'Down this next alley.'

'Mm,' said Nicholas. 'It looks a bit niffy to me.'

The children had never been in the streets behind the shops. The change was abrupt.

'Phew!' said Helen. 'All those fancy windows and posh carpets at the front, and it's a rubbish dump at the back!'

They were in an alley that ran between loading bays and store-houses lit by unshaded bulbs: the kerb was low and had a metal edge, and there was the smell of boxwood and rotten fruit. Fans pumped hot, stale air into the children's faces through vents that were hung with feathers of dirt.

Beyond the alley they came to a warren of grimy streets, where old women stood in the doorways, wearing sacks for aprons, and men in carpet slippers sat on the steps. Dogs nosed among crumpled paper in the gutter; a rusty bicycle wheel lay on the cobbles. A group of boys at the corner talked to a girl whose hair was rolled in brightly coloured plastic curlers.

'I don't like this, Nick,' said Helen. 'Should we go back up the alley?'

'No. They'll think we're scared. Look as though we know where we're going – taking a short cut: something like that.'

As the children walked past, all the eyes in the street watched them, without interest or hostility, but the children felt very uncomfortable, and walked close together. The girl on the corner laughed, but it could have been at something one of the boys had said.

They went on through the streets.

'Perhaps it's not a good idea,' said Roland. 'Shall we go home?'

'Are you lost?' said Nicholas.

'No, but – '

'Now what's all this?' said David.

Ahead of them the streets continued, but the houses were empty, and broken.

'That's queer,' said Nicholas. 'Come on: it looks as though Roland has something after all.'

'Let's go back,' said Roland.

'What, just when it's starting to be interesting? And isn't this the way to your Thursday Street?'

'Well – sort of – yes – I think so.'

'Come on, then.'

It was not one or two houses that were empty, but row after row and street after street. Grass grew in the cobbles everywhere, and in the cracks of the pavement. Doors hung awry. Nearly all the windows were boarded up, or jagged with glass. Only at a few were there any curtains, and these twitched as the children approached. But they saw nobody.

'Isn't it spooky?' said David. 'You feel as if you ought to whisper. What if there was no one anywhere – even when we got back to Piccadilly?'

Helen looked through a window in one of the houses.

'This room's full of old dustbins!' she said.

'What's that chalked on the door?'

'*Leave post at Number Four.*'

'Number Four's empty, too.'

'I shouldn't like to be here at night, would you?' said Helen.

'I keep feeling we're being watched,' said Roland.

'It's not surprising,' said David, 'with all these windows.'

'I've felt it ever since we were at the map in Piccadilly,' said Roland: 'and all the way up Oldham Road.'

'Oh, come off it, Roland,' said Nicholas. 'You're always imagining things.'

'Look there,' said David. 'They've started to bash the houses down. I wonder if we'll see a demolition gang working. They do it with a big iron ball, you know. They swing it from a crane.'

Something had certainly hit the street they were in now, for only the fronts of the houses were standing, and the sky showed on the inside of windows, and staircases led up a patchwork gable end of wallpaper.

At the bottom of the row the children stopped. The streets continued, with cobbles and pavements and lamp posts – but there were no houses, just fields of rubble.

'Where's your Thursday Street now?' said Nicholas.

'There,' said David.

He pointed to a salvaged nameplate that was balanced on a brickheap. 'Thursday Street.'

'You brought us straight here, anyway, Roland,' said Nicholas. 'The whole place has been flattened. It makes you think, doesn't it?'

'There's a demolition gang!' said Helen.

Alone and black in the middle of the wasteland stood a church. It was a plain Victorian building, with buttresses and lancet windows, a steep roof, but no spire. And beside it were a mechanical excavator and a lorry.

'I can't see anybody,' said Roland.

'They'll be inside,' said Nicholas. 'Let's go and ask if we can watch.'

The children set off along what had been Thursday Street. But as they reached the church even Nicholas found it hard to keep up his enthusiasm, for there was neither sound nor movement anywhere.

'We'd hear them if they were working, Nick. They've gone home.'

David turned the iron handle on the door, and pushed. The church clanged as he rattled the heavy latch, but the door seemed to be locked.

'They wouldn't leave all this gear lying around,' said Nicholas. 'They may be having a tea-break or something.'

'The lorry's engine's still warm,' said Roland. 'And there's a jacket in the cab.'

'The tailboard's down, too. They've not finished loading all this wood yet.'

'What is it?'

'Smashed up bits of pews and floorboards.'

'Let's wait, then,' said Nicholas. 'Is there anything else?'

'No – yes there is. There's a ball behind the front wheel.'

'Fetch it out, and we'll have a game.'

Roland pulled a white plastic football from under the lorry: and then he stopped.

'What's the matter?'

'Listen,' said Roland. 'Where's the music coming from?'

'What music? You're hearing things.'

'No: listen, Nick. He's right.'

A fiddle was being played. The notes were thin, and pitched high in a tune of sadness. Away from the children an old man stood alone on the corner of a street, under a broken lamp post. He was poorly dressed, and wore a crumpled hat.

'Why's he playing here?'

'Perhaps he's blind,' said Helen. 'Hadn't we better tell him where he is? He probably thinks there are houses all round him.'

'Blind people know things like that by echoes,' said David. 'Leave him alone: he may be practising. Oh, hurry up, Roland! We're waiting!'

Roland let go of the ball, and kicked it as it fell.

He was about twenty yards from the others, and he punted the ball to reach them on the first bounce: but instead it soared straight from his foot, up and over their heads so quickly that they could hardly follow it. And the ball was still gaining speed, and rising, when it crashed through the middle lancet of the west window of the church.

David whistled. 'Bullseye, Roland! Do it again!'

'Shh!' said Helen.

'It doesn't matter. They're pulling the place down, aren't they?'

'I didn't kick it very hard,' said Roland.

'Not much!'

'Never mind,' said Helen, 'I'll go and see if I can climb in.'

'We'll all go,' said David.

'No. Stay here in case the gang comes back,' said Helen, and she disappeared round the corner of the church.

'Trust you to break a window,' said Nicholas.

'I'm sorry, Nick: I didn't mean to. I just kicked the ball, and it seemed to fly by itself.'

'It flew by itself,' said Nicholas. 'Here we go again!'

'But it did!' said Roland. 'When I kicked the ball, the – the fiddle seemed to stick on a note. Didn't you hear it? It went right through my head. And it got worse and worse, all the time the ball was in the air, until the window broke. Didn't you hear the music?'

'No. And I don't now. And I don't see your fiddler, either. He's gone.'

'There's something odd, though,' said David. 'It was only a plastic ball, but it's snapped the leading in the window.'

'Oh, it was certainly a good kick from old Roland,' said Nicholas. 'And listen: your fiddler's at it again.'

The music was faint, but although the tune was the same as before, it was now urgent, a wild dance; faster; higher; until the notes merged into one tone that slowly rose past the range of hearing. For a while the sound could still be felt. Then there was nothing.

'What's Helen doing?' said Nicholas. 'Hasn't she found it yet?'

'She may not be able to climb in,' said David. 'I'll go and see.'

'And tell her to hurry up,' said Nicholas.

'OK.'

Nicholas and Roland waited.

'I never knew there were places like this, did you, Nick?'

'I think it's what they call "slum clearance",' said Nicholas. 'A lot of the houses were bombed in the war, you know, and those that weren't are being pulled down to make room for new flats. That'll be why all those streets were empty. They're the next for the chop.'

'Where do all the people live while the flats are being built?' said Roland.

'I don't know. But have you noticed? If we'd carried on right across here, the next lot of houses aren't empty. Perhaps those people will move into the flats that are built here. Then that block of streets can be knocked down.'

'There's the fiddle again!' said Roland. It was distant, as before, and fierce. 'But I can't see the old man. Where is he?'

'What's the matter with you today, Roland? Stop dithering: he'll be somewhere around.'

'Yes, but where? He was by the lamp post a second ago, and it's miles to the houses. We couldn't hear him and not see him.'

'I'd rather know where Helen and David have got to,'

said Nicholas. 'If they don't hurry up the gang'll be back before we've found the ball.'

'Do you think they're all right – ?'

'Of course they are. They're trying to have us on.'

'They may be stuck, or locked in,' said Roland.

'They'd have shouted,' said Nicholas. 'No: they're up to something. You wait here, in case they try to sneak out. I'm going to surprise them.'

Roland sat down on a broken kitchen chair that was a part of the landscape. He was cold.

Then the music came again.

Roland jumped up, but there was no fiddler in sight, and he could not make out which direction the sound was coming from.

'Nick!'

The music faded.

'Nick! – Nick!'

The wasteland was bigger in the late afternoon light; the air quiet; and the houses seemed to be painted in the dusk. They were as alien as a coastline from the sea. A long way off, a woman pushed a pram.

'Nick!'

Roland picked his way over the rubble to the other side of the church, and here he found a door which sagged open on broken hinges: two floorboards were nailed across the doorway. Roland climbed through into a passage with several small rooms leading off it. Water trickled from a fractured pipe. There were the smells of soot and cat.

The rooms were empty except for the things that are always left behind. There were some mouldering Sunday school registers; a brass-bound Bible; a faded sepia photograph of the Whitsun procession of 1909; a copy of Kirton's Standard Temperance Reciter, Presented to John Beddowes by the Pendlebury Band of

Hope, February 1888. There was a broken saucer. There was a jam jar furred green with long-dried water.

'Nick!'

Roland went through into the body of the church.

The floorboards and joists had been taken away, leaving the bare earth: everything movable had been ripped out down to the brick. The church was a cavern. Above Roland's head the three lancets of the west window glowed like orange candles against the fading light. The middle lancet, the tallest, was shattered, and the glass lay on the earth. But there was no ball.

'Nick! Helen! David! Where are you?'

The dusk hung like mist in the church.

Roland went back to the passage. At the end was a staircase. The banisters had been pulled out, but the steps remained.

'David! Nick! Come down: please don't hide! I don't like it!'

No one answered. Roland's footsteps thumped on the stairs. Two rooms opened off a landing at the top, and both were empty.

'Nick!'

The echo filled the church.

'Nick!'

Round, and round, his voice went, and through it came a noise. It was low and vibrant, like wind in a chimney. It grew louder, more taut, and the wall blurred, and the floor shook. The noise was in the fabric of the church: it pulsed with sound. Then he heard a heavy door open; and close; and the noise faded away. It was now too still in the church, and footsteps were moving over the rubble in the passage downstairs.

'Who's that?' said Ronald.

The footsteps reached the stairs, and began to climb.

'Who's there?'

Elidor

'Do not be afraid,' said a voice.

'Who are you? What do you want?'

The footsteps were at the top of the stairs. A shadow fell across the landing.

'No!' cried Roland. 'Don't come any nearer!'

The fiddler stood in the doorway.

'I shall not harm you. Take the end of my bow, and lead me. The stairs are dangerous.'

He was bent, and thin: he limped: his voice was old: there looked to be no strength in him: and he was between Roland and the stairs. He stretched out his fiddle bow.

'Help me.'

'All – all right.'

Roland put his hand forward to take the bow, but as he was about to touch it a shock struck his finger tips, driving light through his forehead between the eyes. It was as though a shutter had been lifted in his mind, and in the moment before it dropped again he saw something; but it went so quickly that all he could hold was the shape of its emptiness.

'What did you see?'

'See? I didn't – see. I – through my fingers – See? Towers – like flame. – A candle in darkness. – A black wind.'

'Lead me.'

'Yes.'

Roland went down the stairs, a step at a time, dazed but no longer frightened. The church was somehow remote from him now, and flat, like a piece of stage scenery. The only real things were the fiddler and his bow.

'I heard your music,' said Roland. 'Why were you playing so far away from people?'

'I was near you. Are you not people?' They had

reached the bottom of the stairs, and were standing on the earth floor of the church. 'Give me my bow.'

'I can't stay,' said Roland. But the old man put the fiddle to his shoulder. 'I'm looking for my sister, and my two brothers –' The old man began to play. '– and I must find them before dark –' It was the wild dance. '– and we've a train to catch. What's that noise? – Please! – Stop! – It's hurting! – Please! –'

The air took up the fiddle's note. It was the sound Roland had heard upstairs, but now it was louder, building waves that jarred the church, and went through Roland's body until he felt that he was threaded on the sound.

'– Please! –'

'Now! Open the door!'

'I can't! It's locked!'

'Open it! There is little time!'

'But – !'

'Now!'

Roland stumbled to the door, grasped the iron handle and pulled with all his weight. The door opened, and he ran out on to the cobbles of the street, head down, driven by the noise.

But he never reached the far pavement, for the cobbles were moving under him. He turned. The outline of the church rippled in the air, and vanished. He was standing among boulders on a sea shore, and the music died into the crash of breakers, and the long fall of surf.

2. Cloth of Gold

A cliff rose above him, and at the top were the ruins of a castle. He was confused by the noise that had shaken the church, but the cold thrill and burn of the spray woke him.

Roland walked along the shore. The cliff was an islet separated from the mainland by a channel of foam. High over his head a drawbridge spanned the gap, and there was no other way to cross. He would have to climb, and climb soon, for even as he tried to find the best place to start, a wave dragged at the rocks. The tide was coming in.

The rocks sloped on one side, and were never more than a hard scramble: but the height was bad. The sound of the water dropped away and there was no wind. The cliff thrust him outwards, and each movement felt too violent for him to be able to keep his balance, and the tendons in his wrists were strained by the pressure of his grip on every hold. He knew better than to look down, but once he looked up, and the whole mass of the castle toppled slowly towards him. After that, he forced himself to see only what was within reach of his hand.

The foundations of the castle were smooth masonry curving to the vertical wall, but between the foundations and the bed-rock there was a ledge which Roland worked himself along until he reached the drawbridge.

The chains that raised the bridge had been cut, and he was able to use one of them to pull himself up to the level of the gatehouse. The bridge itself was undamaged, but the gatehouse had fallen in. Roland climbed through into the courtyard.

There were four towers to the castle, one at each corner of the broken walls, and in the middle of the courtyard stood a massive keep. It was high, with few windows.

'Hello!' Roland called.

There was no reply. Roland went through the doorway of the keep into a great hall, cold and dim, and spanned by beams. The floor was strewn with dead roses, and the air heavy with their decay.

An arch in one corner led to a spiral staircase. Here the light came through slits in the wall, and was so poor that for most of the time Roland had to grope his way in darkness.

The first room was an armoury, lined with racks, which held a few swords, pikes, and shields. It took up the whole width of the keep.

Roland drew a sword from one of the racks. The blade was sharp, and well greased. And that was another strange thing about the castle. Although it was a ruin, the scars were fresh. The tumbled stone was unweathered and all the windows held traces of glass.

He replaced the sword: it was too heavy to be of use.

Roland continued up the stairs to the next door. He opened it and looked into a barren room. Shreds of tapestry hung against the walls like the skeletons of leaves, and there was one high window of three lancets . . . and the glass of the middle lancet was scattered on the floor . . . and in the hearth opposite the window lay a white plastic football.

Roland took the ball between his hands, just as he had pulled it from under the lorry. The pattern of stitches: the smear of oil and brick dust: it was the same.

He stared at the ball, and as he stared he heard a man singing. He could not hear the words, but the voice was young, and the tune filled Roland with a yearning that was both pain and gladness in one.

Where's it coming from? he thought. The next room up?

If only he could hear the words. Whoever was singing, he had to hear. But as he moved, the voice stopped.

'No,' whispered Roland.

The ball dropped from his fingers, and for a long time he listened to its slow bounce – bounce – bounce – down – and round – until that was lost.

'He must be up there.'

Roland started to climb. He came to the room above; the last room, for ahead the curve of the stair grew brighter as it opened on to the top of the keep.

There was no one in the room. But under the window stood a low, white, marble table, and draped from one end, as though it had been jerked off, was a tapestry of cloth of gold.

Roland went to the table. It was quite plain, except for

the shape of a sword cut deep in the stone. He picked up the golden tapestry and spread it over the table. It dropped with the folds of long, untouched use, and the impression of the sword was in the cloth. And as he stepped back Roland felt the castle tremble, and the voice drifted to him through the window, far away, but so clear that he caught broken snatches of the words.

> *Fair is this land for all time . . .*
> *Beneath snowfall of flowers . . .*

'O, wait for me!' cried Roland. 'Don't go!'

> *A magic land, and full of song . . .*

He sprang up the steps and on to the battlement of the keep.

> *Green Isle of the Shadow of the Stars.*

All around sea and air mingled to a grey light, and the waves were silver darts on the water. From the drawbridge a road went up towards hills and into a forest that covered the lower slopes. On the road, moving away from the castle, Roland saw the fiddler.

3. Dead Loss

By the time Roland was clear of the gatehouse the fiddler had reached the trees. Roland hurried after him.

For a while the road passed charred stumps of buildings, and fields rank with nettle. Dust, or ash, kicked up under Roland's feet, muffling his walk and coating his body so aridly that his skin rasped. Flies whined round him, and crawled in his hair, and tried to settle on his lips. The sky was dull, yet there was a brittleness in the light that hurt. It was no longer wonder that led him, but dislike of being alone.

Even the singing had lost its enchantment. For now that the old man had appeared again Roland recognised where he had heard the song before: the fiddler had played it. And so what he had imagined to be the music of his dreams was only the jingle of a half-learned tune.

Although Roland wanted to catch up with the man, he wanted less and less to reach the forest. He could make out nothing sinister at first, apart from a general atmosphere of gloom and stillness, and it was not until he was close that he knew why this forest was different from all others. The trees were dead.

Roland looked back: but he had nowhere else to go, and at that distance the castle was a tortured crag. He clutched a handful of gravel and rubbed it against his cheek. It hurt. It was real. He was there. He had only himself.

Within the forest the road dwindled to a line of mud that strayed wherever there was ground to take it: fungus glowed in the twilight, and moss trailed like hair from the branches. There was the silence of death over everything: a silence that was more powerful for the noises it contained – the far off crash of trees, and the voices of cold things hidden in the fog that moved in ribbons where there was no wind. Oaks became black water at a touch.

Roland could not tell how long he had struggled, nor how far, when the trees thinned on to moorland below a skyline of rock. The forest held neither hours nor miles, and all that he had been able to do was to wade from one bog into the next, to climb over one rotting trunk to the next, and to hope for an end to the slime.

He walked a few shambling steps clear of the trees, and collapsed in the grass. He had lost the road, and he was alone.

When he opened his eyes Roland thought that he would never move again. The chill had seeped through his body and locked him to the ground.

He turned on to his side, and dragged himself to a sitting position, his head on his knees, too cold to shiver.

However long he had slept, nothing had changed. The light was just the same, the sky unbroken.

He began to walk uphill towards the rocks. They were higher than he had thought – packed columns of granite, splintered by frost and ribbed by wind – but he scrambled amongst them up weathered gullies to the top.

Here Roland found himself on a broad ridge shelving away to a plain which stretched into the haze. Nothing showed. No villages; no houses; no light; no smoke. He was alone. Behind him the hill dropped to the forest, and he could see no end to that. The only proof that anyone had ever lived in this land was close by him, but it gave Roland little comfort.

A circle of standing stones crowned the hill. They were unworked and top-heavy; three times bigger than a man

and smooth as flint. They rose from the ground like
clenched fists. Roland walked into the circle which was
easily four hundred yards wide, and at the middle he
stopped and gazed round him.

From the circle an avenue of stones marched along
the ridge, and these were sharp blades of rock, as tall as
the circle, but cruel and thin. They went straight to a
round hill, a mile away.

If possible, the air was quieter here: so quiet that
it was as if the silence lay in Roland. He avoided
making any noise, for fear that the stillness would not be
broken.

But how many stones were there in the circle? Roland
started to count from the left of the avenue – Eighty-eight.
Or did he miss one right at the end? Try again – eighty-
five, eighty-six, eighty-seven. It may have been that his

eyes were tired, but the flick, flick, flick, flick, flick of
the pale shapes as he counted them was making the
stones in the corner of his vision seem to move – eighty-
four, eighty-five, eighty-six, eighty-seven, eighty-eight,
eighty-nine. Just once more. One, two, three, five, six –
No. One, two, three, four, five, six, seven – The air was
like a deafness about him.

Why am I bothering to count? thought Roland.

'You must stay until you have counted them all.'

Yes, I must – who said that? Roland caught himself
looking over his shoulder.

I did. I must be cracked.

The silence was so complete that his thought had
sounded as loud as a voice.

I'm getting out of this.

Roland sprinted across the circle, intent only on reach-
ing the open hill-top, and he did not notice at first that
he was running into the mouth of the avenue. He
swerved aside towards a gap between the stones, but as
he approached, the perspective seemed to alter, to become reversed, so that instead of growing broader the
gap appeared to shrink. He could not pass through.

Roland changed direction, bewildered by his mis-
judgment of distance – and now he was going into the
avenue again. Eighty-six. Eighty-seven. Eighty-eight.
Eighty-nine. Ninety. Stones don't move. There's plenty
of room between them.

He fixed his eyes on one gap, and made for it.

These huge boulders were spaced many times their
own width apart, yet as Roland drew near, instinct told
him that the gap was not wide enough. He kept jerking
back, as though from an unseen obstacle in the dark.
Stones – don't – move. There's plenty – of room. He
could see that there was, but even in the last yard he

flinched from the stones, and the moment of passing
through tore a great, wordless cry from his throat.

'I'm imagining things,' said Roland.

The abruptness with which his fear had left him was
frightening in itself, for the instant Roland crossed out
of the circle the stones shrank in his mind to their true
size.

'You could drive a bus between them!'

But even so, the air was less stifled now, and nothing
moved when he counted. – Eighty-one. Again. – Eighty-
one. No trouble at all.

Roland decided to follow the avenue to the hill. He
would have a better view from there, and perhaps
something would give direction to his wandering: but
he kept well clear of the standing stones, walking below
them on the ridge.

It soon became obvious that the hill, for all its mass,
was not a part of the ridge but an artificial mound,
completely circular, and flat-topped.

The avenue ended at a dry moat, or ditch, that went
round the hill. Roland slithered into the ditch, ran across
its broad floor, and started to climb. The turf was like
glass under his shoes.

From the top of the mound there was one landmark,
in front of him on the plain, far off.

A heap of rocks. No, thought Roland, it's towers – and
walls: all broken. Another castle. That's not much use.
What else?

Roland screwed up his eyes, and after a while he
thought he could make out a form that was more sub-
stantial than the shifting clouds, away to his left.

A castle. Black. Dead loss. – There's got to be something.

But the view showed only desolation. Plain, ridge,

forest, sea, all were spent. Even colour had been drained from the light, and Roland saw everything, his own flesh and clothes, in shades of grey, as if in a photograph.

Three castles.

He looked to his right. Here the dark was like thunder, impenetrable. Then – It came, and went, and came again.

It's a light. On a hill. Very faint – like – a – candle – dying – Towers! Golden towers!

Roland could never remember whether he saw it, or whether it was a picture in his mind, but as he strained to pierce the haze, his vision seemed to narrow and to draw the castle towards him. It shone as if the stones had soaked in light, as if stone could be amber. People were moving on the walls: metal glinted. Then clouds drifted over.

Roland was back on the hill-top, but that spark in the mist across the plain had driven away the exhaustion, the hopelessness. It was the voice outside the keep: it was a tear of the sun.

He started for the castle at once. He crabbed down, braking with his hands. It would be all right now. It would be all right: all right now. He landed in a heap at the bottom of the mound. Close by his head four fingers of a woollen glove stuck out of the turf.

Four fingers of a woollen glove pointing out of the mound, and the turf grew smooth between each finger, without a mark on it.

Roland crept his hand forward and – the glove was empty. He dragged a penknife out of his pocket and began to hack at the turf. The root mantle lay only two inches deep on white quartz, and he cut back and peeled the turf like matting. It came in a strip, a fibrous mould of the glove below, with four neat holes. The fingers and the cuff were free, but the thumb went straight into the quartz.

Roland looked for the name tape inside the cuff. He found it: Helen R. Watson.

He stabbed the turf, but he could find no break in the quartz, nothing that he could lift. The glove was fused into the rock. There were no cracks, no lesions. The thumb went into unflawed rock, and turf had covered it.

Roland jerked the glove, but he could not move it. He threw his weight against it in all directions, and the glove twisted and swung him to his knees. He wrestled, but the glove dragged him down in exhaustion, hand-cuffed to the mound.

He knelt, his head on his forearm, looking at the quartz: white: cold: hard: clean. – But a stain was growing over it, his shadow, blacker and blacker. The light was changing. And from the drift of the shadow Roland knew that the cause of the brightness was moving up close behind him.

4. Malebron

It was a man with yellow hair. He wore a golden cloak, a golden shield on his arm. In his hand was a spear, and its head was like flame.

'Is there light in Gorias?' he said.

'Help me,' said Roland. 'The glove.'

'Is there light?' said the man.

'The glove,' said Roland. 'Helen.'

He could think of nothing, do nothing. His head rang with heartbeats, and the hill spun. He lay on the turf. And slowly a quietness grew, like sleep, and in the quietness he could hold the glove so that it was not a grappling hand. The man stood, unmoving, and the words came back to Roland as he had heard them before the table of the cloth of gold. The table: the castle: and the man – nothing else showed the colour of life in all this wasted land.

The man's face was slender, with high cheekbones, and the locks of his hair swept backwards as if in a wind.

'Who are you?' whispered Roland.

'Malebron of Elidor.'

'What's that?' said Roland.

'Is there light in Gorias?'

'I don't understand,' said Roland.

The man began to climb the hill, but he was lame. One foot dragged. He did not look to see whether Roland was following.

'Are you hurt?' said Roland.

'Wounds do not heal in Elidor.'

'There was a fiddler,' said Roland. 'He'd got a bad leg. I had to help him –'

'Now that you have come,' said Malebron, 'I need
not skulk, in beggar's rags again. Look.' They were at the
top of the mound. He pointed to the distant ruined keep.

'There is Findias, Castle of the South. And the forest,
Mondrum: the fairest wood in Elidor.'

'It was you?' said Roland. 'You? Then you must have
been watching me all the time! You just dumped me by
the cliff – and left me – and what have you done with
Helen? And David and Nick? What's happened?'
shouted Roland.

But his voice had no power in the air, and Malebron
waited, ignoring him, until Roland stopped.

'And Falias, and Murias,' he said. 'Castles of the West
and of the North. There on the plain beneath.'

He spoke the names of castle and wood as if they were
precious things, not three black fangs and a swamp.

'But Gorias, in the east – what did you see?'

'I – saw a castle,' said Roland. 'It was all golden – and
alive. Then I saw the glove. She –'

'You have known Mondrum, and those ravaged
walls,' said Malebron: 'the grey land, the dead sky. Yet
what you saw in Gorias once shone throughout Elidor,
from the Hazel of Fordruim, to the Hill of Usna. So we
lived, and no strife between us. Now only in Gorias is
there light.'

'But where's – ?' said Roland.

'The darkness grew,' said Malebron. 'It is always
there. We did not watch, and the power of night closed
on Elidor. We had so much of ease that we did not mark
the signs – a crop blighted, a spring failed, a man killed.
Then it was too late – war, and siege, and betrayal, and
the dying of the light.'

'Where's Helen?' said Roland.

Malebron was silent, then he said quietly, 'A maimed
king and a mumbling boy! Is it possible?'

'I don't know what you're talking about,' said Roland. 'Where's Helen? That's her glove, and the thumb's stuck in the rock.'

'Gloves!' cried Malebron. 'Look about you! I have endured, and killed, only in the belief that you would come. And you have come. But you will not speak to me of gloves! You will save this land! You will bring back light to Elidor!'

'Me!'

'There is no hope but you.'

'Me,' said Roland. 'I'm no use. What could I do?'

'Nothing,' said Malebron, 'without me. And without you, I shall not live. Alone, we are lost: together, we shall bring the morning.'

'All this,' said Roland, 'was like the golden castle – like you sang? The whole country?'

'All,' said Malebron.

'– Me?'

'You.'

Findias . . . Falias . . . Murias . . . Gorias. The Hazel of Fordruim . . . the Forest of Mondrum . . . the Hill of Usna. Men who walked like sunlight. Cloth of gold. Elidor. – Elidor.

Roland thought of the gravel against his cheek. This is true: now: I'm here. And only I can do it. He says so. He says I can bring it all back. Roland Watson, Fog Lane, Manchester 20. What about that? Now what about that!

'How do you know I can?' said Roland.

'I have watched you prove your strength,' said Malebron. 'Without that strength you would not have lived to stand here at the heart of the darkness.'

'Here?' said Roland. 'It's just a hill –'

'It is the Mound of Vandwy,' said Malebron. 'Night's dungeon in Elidor. It has tried to destroy you. If you had not been strong you would never have left the stone circle. But you were strong, and I had to watch you prove your strength.'

'I don't see how a hill can do all this,' said Roland. 'You can't fight a hill.'

'No,' said Malebron. 'We fight our own people. Darkness needs no shape. It uses. It possesses. This Mound and its stones are from an age long past, yet they were built for blood, and were supple to evil.'

Roland felt cold and small on the hill.

'I've got to find the others first,' he said.

'It is the same thing,' said Malebron.

'No, but they'll be better than me: they're older. And I've got to find them, anyway.'

'It is the same thing,' said Malebron. 'Listen. You have seen Elidor's four castles. Now each castle was built to guard a Treasure, and each Treasure holds the light of Elidor. They are the seeds of flame from which all this land was grown. But Findias and Falias and Murias are taken, and their Treasures lost.

'You are to save these Treasures. Only you can save them.'

'Where are they?' said Roland. 'And you said there were four Treasures: so where's the other?'

'I hold it,' said Malebron. 'The Spear of Ildana from Gorias. Three castles lie wasted: three Treasures are in the Mound. Gorias stands. You will go to Vandwy, and you will bring back light to Elidor.'

5. The Mound of Vandwy

They were at the foot of the Mound.

'How do we get in?' said Roland.

'Through the door.'

'What door? It's just turf.'

'That is why you are here,' said Malebron. 'The door is hidden, but you can find it.'

'How?' said Roland.

'Make the door appear: think it: force it with your mind. The power you know fleetingly in your world is here as real as swords. We have nothing like it. Now close your eyes. Can you still see the Mound in your thought?'

'Yes.'

'There is a door in the Mound,' said Malebron. 'A door.'

'What kind of door?' said Roland.

'It does not matter. Any door. The door you know best. Think of the feel of it. The sound of it. A door. The door. The only door. It must come. Make it come.'

Roland thought of the door at the new house. He saw the blisters in the paint, and the brass flap with 'Letters' outlined in dry metal polish. He had been cleaning it only yesterday. It was a queer door to be stuck in the side of a hill.

'I can see it.'

'Is it there? Is it firm? Could you touch it?' said Malebron.

'I think so,' said Roland.

'Then open your eyes. It is still there.'

'No. It's just a hill.'

'It is still there!' cried Malebron. 'It is real! You have made it with your mind! Your mind is real! You can see the door!'

Roland shut his eyes again. The door had a brick porch, and there was a house leek growing on the stone roof. His eyes were so tightly closed that he began to see coloured lights floating behind his lids, and they were all shaped like the porch entrance. There was no need to think of it now – he could see nothing else but these miniature, drifting arches: and behind them all, unmoving, the true porch, square-cut, solid.

'The Mound must break! It cannot hide the door!'

'Yes,' said Roland. 'It's there. The door. It's real.'

'Then look! Now!'

Roland opened his eyes, and he saw the frame of the porch stamped in the turf, ghostly on the black hill. And as he looked the frame quivered, and without really changing, became another door; pale as moonlight, grey as ashwood; low; a square, stone dolmen arch made of three slabs – two upright and a lintel. Below it was a step carved with spiral patterns that seemed to revolve without moving. Light spread from the doorway to Roland's feet.

'The door will be open as long as you hold it in your memory,' said Malebron.

'Aren't you coming?' said Roland.

'No. That light is death in Elidor. It will not harm you, but be ready. We have word of something merciless here, though we do not know what it is.'

Beyond the dolmen arch a straight and level passage went into the hill.

'You will wait?' said Roland.

'I shall wait.'

'I'm frightened.'

The idea of stopping into that narrow opening in the ground choked his breath. He would be hemmed in by rock, the walls leaned, and there would be earth piled over his head, earth on top of him, pressing him down, crushing him. The walls would crush him. He tasted clay in his mouth.

'I can't do it,' he said. 'I can't go in. Take me back. It's nothing to do with me. It's your world, and it's all dead.'

'No!' said Malebron. 'Gorias lives!'

But the golden castle was shrouded in Roland's mind, and its flames were too far away to warm the pallor of the Mound.

'Find someone else! Not me! It's nothing to do with me!'

'It is,' said Malebron. 'Our worlds are different, but they are linked in subtle ways, and the death of Elidor would not be without its echo in your world.'

'I don't care! It's nothing to do with me!'

'It is,' said Malebron. His voice was hard. 'Your sister and your brothers are in the Mound.'

Roland saw the glove lying, free now, below the grey spirals.

'They went, each in their turn,' said Malebron. 'Time is different here.'

'What's happened to them?' said Roland.

'They have failed. But you are stronger than any of them.'

'I'm not.'

'Here, in Elidor, you are stronger.'

'Do you mean that?' said Roland.

'Much stronger. You will go.'

'Yes,' said Roland. Now that there was no choice the panic left him.

'Take this spear,' said Malebron. 'The last Treasure for the last chance. It will give comfort beyond the temper of its blade.'

Roland held the spear. Fires moved deep in the metal, and its edge was a rainbow.

'What are the other Treasures?' said Roland.

'A sword, a cauldron, and a stone. Except these, trust nothing. And do not think twice to use the spear: for little you may meet in Vandwy can be good.'

The light in the Mound was white and soft, and appeared to come from nowhere, which made the passage indistinct, without texture or shadows. There was nothing on which Roland could focus. Sometimes he felt that he was not moving; at others that he had travelled a long way – much farther than was possible if he had gone straight into the Mound. When he looked back the doorway was lost in the thick light.

And he became aware of a sound; or rather the memory of a sound. It was not loud enough for him to hear, but he kept shaking his head to break the rhythm of five or six notes, many times repeated, like drops of water. And he noticed small changes in the fabric of the light, less than the shimmering of silk, but they were keeping time with this pure, soulless beauty that he could not hear.

And still the passage continued. Roland was worried now. Something was wrong, or he had lost all his sense of bearing.

'Where's the end?' he said aloud, more to hear his voice than to ask a question. But then he stopped. As he had spoken the words there had been a brief flaw in the light, a blemish that was gone the moment it came.

'The end of the tunnel,' said Roland.

It came again; a triangle of light, within the light; an arch.

'The – end – of – the – tunnel.'

Roland hung on to the thought with all his will, and again the arch appeared, more fixed now.

'Stay – there.'

He could breathe without its trembling, and as he moved it drew nearer, and was rooted in stone, and he came out into a round chamber shaped like a bee-hive.

'Helen!'

She was sitting with David and Nicholas on the floor of the chamber, and all three were staring upwards.

'Touch it, Roland,' said Nicholas. 'Listen to it.'

'It's the loveliest sound,' said Helen.

'I want to hear it again,' said David.

Their voices were without tone or feeling.

Roland looked up.

It was the most delicate, the most wonderful thing he had ever seen.

A thread hung from the dome, and at the end of it

was a branch of apple blossom. The branch was silver,
and the blossom of crystal. The veins in the leaves and
petals were like spun mercury.

'It's beautiful!' said Roland.

'Touch the flowers, Roland.'

'They make music when you touch them.'

'The loveliest music.'

'It's beautiful!' said Roland.

'Touch them.'

'The flowers.'

'Touch.'

The branch was so still that it seemed to move under
Roland's gaze, and there was a fragrance of sound all
about him, a music that he could not quite hear, a fading
harmony of petals.

'Touch them, Roland.'

If he touched them they would sing, and the music
would be unlocked from the crystal, and he would
hear . . .

'Touch.'

If he could reach them. The branch was coming
nearer. If he stood on tip-toe, and stretched upwards
with his spear.

But as Roland lifted the spear flecks of yellow light
crackled round its head, and he pulled back his arm,
tingling with shock.

'Touch the flowers, Roland.'

'You touch them!' said Roland. 'Why don't you? You
can't!'

He looked up again. The branch was dropping towards him on its thread like a spider.

'I'll touch them!' cried Roland, and he swung the
spear.

The air burst round him as discords of sound that
crashed from wall to wall, and died away, and every-

thing went black. Helen screamed, but it was Helen, and not a mindless voice.

'Where are you?' said Nicholas.

'There's a light,' said David.

'It's my spear,' said Roland. 'I'll hold it up. Are you hurt?'

'We're OK,' said Nicholas. They all made towards the spear, and crouched together round it. 'What's happening?'

'We're in the hill,' said Roland. 'Don't you remember?'

'Hill?' said David. 'Yes – the Treasures. And Malebron. But there was light –'

'I smashed the apple branch.'

'An apple branch – I looked at it. I touched it – I – can't remember.'

'The Treasures,' said Roland. 'Did you find the Treasures?'

'No.'

'What's that?' said Helen. 'Over there.'

'And there,' said David. 'And on the other side, too.'

They were growing used to the spear light, and they could just make out the wall of the rock chamber. There were four arches in it. One was black, the passage mouth: but the others shone faintly.

'I'll keep a look out here,' said Roland. 'You go and see what they are.'

'This one's a small room,' said Helen.

'So's this –'

Shadows flapped in the chamber like bats as the children stooped through the arches. And for a time all was silence. Roland stood alone by the entrance to the passage, holding the spear upright on the floor. Then the shadows began to move again, and towards him from the archways, slowly and without a word, the other three came and the darkness shrank before them.

In David's hand was a naked sword. The blade was like ice, and the hilt all jewels and fire.

Nicholas held a stone, golden, that seemed to be burning inside.

And Helen was carrying a bowl – a cauldron, with pearls about the rim. And as she walked, light splashed and ran through her fingers like water.

6. The Lay of the Starved Fool

'But how did we come through from the church to the castle?' said David.

The children sat by Malebron on the ridge, clear of the hill. The dolmen arch was drab with lichen, and the stones of the avenue heeled like twisted palings. Clouds still rolled upon the plain, but there was a quickening in the air, and Findias, Falias, and Murias were etched in gold, as though they stood before the dawn.

'It is not easy to cross from your world into this,' said Malebron, 'but there are places where they touch. The church, and the castle. They were battered by war, and now all the land around quakes with destruction. They have been shaken loose in their worlds.'

'But the fiddle: and the noise – what was that?' said Roland.

'All things have their note, and will answer to it.'

'You mean, like a wine-glass ringing?'

'Yes,' said Malebron. 'And when the church answered, it existed in both places at once – the real church, and the echo of itself. Yet more than echo, for although you opened the door here, no door opened in your world.'

'Can you always do this?' said Helen.

'No. The finding is chance. Wasteland and boundaries: places that are neither one thing nor the other, neither here nor there – these are the gates of Elidor.'

'Isn't it funny how things happen?' said Roland. 'You know: if we hadn't gone into Manchester today, and if we hadn't played that game with the map, and if the demolition gang hadn't had a tea-break – all these little things happening at just the right time – all ending like this.'

The children looked at the four Treasures, sword, stone, spear, and cauldron, glowing in their hands.

'One each,' said David.

'Yes,' said Malebron. And he took the fiddle and bow from under his cloak. They were slung on a cord across his shoulder, and there was also a pouch fastened to the cord. He opened it, and took out an oblong package, and began to unwrap layer after layer of very thin oiled cloth. He smoothed each layer, and put it aside, before peeling off the next.

It was an old book, made of vellum. The leaves were hard, glossy, and crimped with age. Malebron opened the book and held it out for the children to see.

Nothing that had yet happened to Roland compared with the shock of this moment.

He was looking at a page of script written in a language that was unknown to him. And at the top of the page was a picture of himself, with Helen, Nicholas, and David by his side. The figures were stiff and puppet-like, and everything was out of scale, but there was no mistaking them. They stood close together, cradling the Treasures in their arms, their heads tilted to one side, a blank expression on their faces, their toes pointing downwards. Next to them was a round hill with a dolmen in its side, and by it another figure, smaller than the children: Malebron. His arms were spread wide, and he held the fiddle in one hand and the bow in the other.

'We've even got the right Treasures,' said Roland. For in the picture he had a spear; and David, the sword: Helen, the cauldron; Nicholas, the stone.

Malebron put his finger on the script, and read:

'*And they shall come from the waves.*
And the Glory of Elidor shall pass with them.
And the Darkness shall not fade.
Unless there is heard the Song of Findhorn.
Who walks in the High Places.'

'But who wrote it?' said David. 'And how did he know?'

'This book was written so long ago,' said Malebron, 'that we have only legend to tell us about it.

'The legend says that there was once a ploughboy in Elidor: an idiot, given to fits. But in his fit he spoke clearly, and was thought to prophesy. And he became so famous that he was taken into the king's household, where he swore that he would starve among plenty, and so it happened: for he was locked in a pantry, and died there.

'However it was, his prophecies were written in this book, which is called *The Lay of the Starved Fool*.

'Through the years it has been read only for its nonsense. But when the prophecies started to be fulfilled, when the first darkness crept into Elidor, I saw in *The Lay of the Starved Fool* not nonsense, but the confused fragments of a dream: a dream that no sane man could bear to dream: a waking memory of what was to be.

'Since then I have worked to discover the truth hidden in the Lay, because, you see, I knew nothing of what I have just told you about our two worlds. I have had to find out that for myself by trial and thought, by asking all the time: how is this true, and if it is true, how can it be?

'Do you understand, then, what it was to find the note that made the church answer, to watch Findias dissolve, to step through into your world, and to see you whom I have known for so long running towards me across the broken land?'

'It's as if everything that's ever happened was leading up to this,' said Roland. 'You can't say how far back it started: everything working together: like cog wheels. When I spun the street names they had to stop at that one place –'

That had been the moment when he had felt that he was being watched.

'Remember, I have said the worlds are linked,' said Malebron. 'And what you have done here will be reflected in some way, at some time, in your world.'

'Wait a minute,' said Roland. 'Will you read us that bit out of the book again?'

And they shall come from the waves.
And the Glory of Elidor shall pass with them.
And the Darkness shall not fade.
Unless there is heard the Song of Findhorn.
Who walks in the High Places.

'We've been going on as though we've saved Elidor, and now that you've found the Treasures you'll be all right,' said Roland. 'But doesn't the book mean that things'll be worse, not better?'

'It does,' said Malebron. 'We are not at the end but at the beginning. But with the Treasures we may hold Gorias, and from there win back to the other castles. Then we shall have four islands in the darkness, and some of us may yet see Mondrum green.'

'But who's Findhorn?' said Roland.

'No one knows,' said Malebron. 'There are desolate mountains far to the north, at the edge of the world, where in the old days it was thought that demons lived. I think these are the High Places. But Findhorn and the Song are forgotten, and now that the Treasures are safe I can go to look for him there. I have proved the wisdom of the Starved Fool now, and that gives me the courage to prove it once again.'

They climbed down from the ridge into Mondrum, and made their way back towards Findias through the slime. The journey seemed much shorter to Roland than when he had been alone, or perhaps it was because Malebron knew where he was going and led them straight there.

The Treasures surrounded them in a field of colour which moved with them, so that as they came to a tree it would change from grey, to purple, to the livid colours of decay, and then sink back into the dead light when they had passed by.

They saw nothing of Findias until they reached the open ground below the forest half a mile from the castle, and at this distance the golden outline did not show. But the ruins were clear in detail, as though the children and Malebron were looking at them through a hole in a dirty window pane.

When they were nearly at the drawbridge Roland turned for a last sight of Elidor.

'Malebron? Something's happened – on the ridge.'

They could just see the ridge above the trees, and the squat cone of Vandwy, with the avenue leading from it. The standing stones of the avenue, which they had left in disorder, were now upright, sharp, harsh, and menacing. And as they watched, a dark beam like a black searchlight leapt from the Mound.

'Run!' shouted Malebron. 'I have been too proud, and Vandwy has recovered from its wound!'

The beam circled, sweeping land and sky, and before the children reached the drawbridge it caught them, and locked on to them beyond escape.

The air was as thick as water. It dragged about their limbs and clogged their lungs, and was shot through with strands of blackness which their hands could not feel or push aside, but each strand plucked at their minds like wire as they blundered through.

'Think of suns! – Meadows, and bright flowers! – Think! – Do not let night into your minds!'

Malebron walked beside the children, urging, driving them on. He moved freely, untouched by the dark.

'Your strength is your weakness now! Vandwy has sent Fear to be given shape by you! These shapes will be real, as the door was real! Keep them out!'

But the fear was in the children: a numbness that sapped the will. And soon they began to hear in the forest the pursuit that they themselves were making.

Slowly they crossed the bridge. But those few yards were longer than the whole journey. The children's vision was so blighted by the strands that they saw the bridge shoot out like a pier over the sea, and the castle was a speck where the lines of the planks converged in the distance.

The bridge became higher and narrower: and then it was tilted to the left: and then to the right: and then upwards, so that they could not walk: and then down, so that they were on a wooden precipice and dared not move: and then the bridge swung completely over, and they felt that they would drop off into the sky. And all the time Malebron fought for their minds.

'The – bridge – is – safe! You – will – not – stop! Think! Move!'

They reached the gatehouse. And as they laboured through to the courtyard there bounded from the forest something that was on two legs but was not a man, and behind it the trees ran howling.

The children fell into the courtyard, and the grip of Vandwy slackened.

'Take the Treasures!' said Malebron.

'No! You need them!'

'We are trapped. Take them to your world and guard them there. They will be safe. And while they are free their light will not die in Elidor, and we may live.'

'Come with us!' said Helen.

'I cannot. I must seal the gate. Nothing must follow you through the keep: stand well clear on the other side.'

'What shall we do with the Treasures?' said Roland.

'No more than guard them. And if we fail here, the light of Elidor may live on, and kindle again in other worlds.'

Malebron put the fiddle to his shoulder and began to play: faster and faster, until the notes merged and drove through the children, cutting the darkness from their minds, snapping the threads of Vandwy with the pain. The keep picked up the fiddle's note, and the surface of the stone lost its hardness, rippled like skin.

'Now go!' cried Malebron. 'Go!'

The ramparts by the gatehouse bristled with silhouettes.

'Malebron!'

'Go!'

The children staggered through the doorway of the keep. The ground shook so much that they could hardly stand: their teeth burred in their heads, the walls were a fog of sound, plaster came like snow from the ceiling. A gap appeared in front of them, and they pulled and pushed each other towards it and between two floor-boards that were nailed across the gap, and ran, choking, out on to the wasteland of Thursday Street.

The fiddle note held. Each brick in the derelict church was grinding against the next. Mortar dust spouted from the joints.

'Look out!' Nicholas yelled. 'It's going!'

All the sounds rose together to one unbearable pitch, the wall bellied outwards, and the church fell in a groaning roar of destruction.

'Roland! The Treasures! What's happened to them?'

But Roland was gazing at the tangled ruin of the church, and could not answer.

'It's all right,' he said at last. 'It's all right. We'll be able to hide them now.'

The children stood before the rubble as the dust cleared. It was late afternoon. A long way off, a woman pushed a pram.

In his hand Roland held a length of iron railing; Nicholas a keystone from the church. David had two splintered laths nailed together for a sword; and Helen an old, cracked cup, with a beaded pattern moulded on the rim.

7. Corporation Property

'We couldn't have looked after them as they were,' said Roland.

The children became aware of voices shouting. Several men had come out of a corner shop in a street on the edge of the wasteland and were running towards the church. But no one moved: it seemed to have nothing to do with them.

'I'll have yez! I'll have yez this time!'

The men were white with fear. The first one to arrive grabbed Nicholas by the back of his collar and swung him round.

'Was there any of yez in there?' he shouted.

'Let go,' said Nicholas.

'Yez'll answer me! Was there any of yez in there?'

'Righto, Paddy, that's enough,' said the biggest of the men. He wore a leather belt covered with regimental badges, and appeared to be the foreman.

'Now then,' he said, speaking to all the children. 'I want a straight answer. Was there any of you in there when she dropped?'

'No,' said Nicholas.

The foreman sagged with relief, and the colour rose in his face. Now he could afford to be angry.

'I've given you kids round here warning time and again,' he said, 'but you'll not learn, will you? You'll not be satisfied till one of you's killed. Well, it's going to stop. Your parents can't manage you, seemingly, so we'll see what the police can do.'

'We've never been here –' said Nicholas.

'Now then,' said the foreman. 'We want none of your lip.'

'Eh, guv'nor,' said the Irishman holding Nicholas. 'Do you not think a good thumpin' might be better?'

'No, Pad, you can't go on treating kids soft. Round here they think kindness is weakness. And something's got to be done. You know how it'd be the first time one of 'em was hurt, don't you? "Gross Negligence on the Firm's Part": that's what. "Insufficient Precautions", and the like. And no mention of all we have to contend with. No mention of "Malicious Damage Endangering Safety of Staff": "Damage to Tools and Plant": "Theft". Eh, Jack: just have a look round while we're at it.'

'Righ',' said a boy wearing a tartan cap, jeans, and mud-covered, pointed shoes. He started to check the tools.

'No: it's all 'ere – wait on! Someone's pinched me football!'

'Well?' said the foreman.

'I'm sorry,' said Roland. 'It's – it's in there.'

'Indeed,' said the foreman.

'I kicked it through the window, and we went in to fetch it.'

'Six bob it cost!' said Jack.

'We haven't any money on us,' said David, 'but we'll send you a postal order.'

'Oh, ay?'

'An example, that's what's going to be made of you,' said the foreman. 'An example. I suppose you know nothing about the lead that went missing from the roof last night, do you?'

'Of course not,' said Nicholas.

' "Of course not." Ay, well, we'll see, shan't we? Now drop those bits of scrap you've got in your hands, and come along. It's the police station for you. Keep fast of that biggest, Pad: he'll be the ringleader.'

'There's no need,' said Nicholas. 'We'll go with you. It's all a mistake.'

'It is that,' said the foreman. 'Now drop that stuff.'

'No,' said Roland.

'You what?'

'We've not stolen them. They're ours.'

'Now look: I'm not here to argue,' said the foreman. 'Put those things back where you found them.'

'They're not yours,' said Roland.

' "Unlawful Possession of Corporation Property",' said the foreman, 'as well as "Trespass" and "Wilful Damage". It's not funny, me lad.'

There were five men, and Jack. They were strong, but heavily built. Jack was the only one who looked capable of any speed.

'Remember what happened to the apple branch?' Roland said to Nicholas.

'Er – yes,' said Nicholas.

'Are you sure?'

'Yes.'

'Right!' said Roland, and he swung the length of railing up against the Irishman's elbow, down and sideways across Jack's shins, and ran.

Through the din that broke out behind him he could hear both the clump of wellingtons and much lighter footsteps, but soon the wellingtons faded.

'Keep going!' shouted Helen. 'We're all here! And the Treasures!'

The children stopped when they reached the first of the streets. Only three of the men had made any effort to catch them but they had given up and were now going back to join the foreman, who was waving his arms at the Irishman and Jack.

'I hope they're all right,' said Roland. 'But there
wasn't anything else to do, was there? I mean, we
couldn't tell them, could we?'

'If you've any sense,' said Nicholas, 'you won't tell
anybody; ever; unless you want locking up.'

'Do you think they really will fetch the police?' said
Helen.

'I doubt it,' said Nicholas. 'Not now they've lost us.
But let's be moving – just in case.'

It was dark when the children reached Oldham Road,
and rushing crowds filled the pavement.

'It's lucky we want to go this way!' shouted Helen,
and vanished behind a wedge of men all wearing bowlers

hats. She reappeared, her cup held at chin height to avoid being smashed.

David and Roland had less trouble with their laths and railing, apart from a few angry grunts from people who came too near. But Nicholas was struggling with his keystone, shifting it from one hip to the other, and he was grey about the mouth.

The pressure of the crowd eased as they came to the station forecourt.

'There's a train in ten minutes,' said Helen.

The crowd split at the barriers. Nicholas wobbled on one leg, balancing the stone on his knee, while he felt in his pocket for the tickets.

'Here, David,' he said. 'You take them.'

David handed the tickets to the ticket collector, who was so busy with his punch that he never looked up – until he noticed David.

'What's all this here?' he said.

'They're our tickets,' said David.

'Ay, happen they are. But you don't think you're fit to travel on a train in that state, do you?'

The children looked at themselves.

They were all coated with slime from the forest of Mondrum and on that was laid plaster, soot, and brick dust from the church.

'We'll stand,' said David.

'You will not,' said the ticket collector.

'But we've paid.'

A restless queue was building up: people were muttering, stamping, looking at watches.

'Clear off,' said the ticket collector. 'And take your junk with you. I don't know how you've the cheek to try it on. There's a copper by the book stall – must I give him a shout? Eh? I thought not. Go on. Off with you.'

The children slipped out of the queue and round the corner from the policeman.

'What do we do now?' said Helen.

'Move along to platform eleven,' said Roland. 'We can cross on to our platform over the bridge at the far end.'

'But no one'll let us through,' said Helen.

'No one'll see us,' said Roland. 'It's the platform where parcel vans go, and there's an entrance for them next to the barrier.'

'We'll still be seen.'

'They're too busy to be watching all that closely. Next time one of those trolleys comes along pulling mail bags walk beside it, and keep your heads down, and then once we're through, nip over into the crowd.'

'There,' said Roland a few minutes later. 'It was easy.'

'You've some nerve,' said Nicholas. 'Where's it come from all of a sudden?'

'You were pretty glad of it this afternoon,' said David.

'Have you thought what'll be said at home?'

'Gosh, no,' said Nicholas. 'That's serious, isn't it? I tell you what: you and I'll wash in one lavatory on the train, and Helen and Roland in the other. There are always two in the last coach.'

'OK. But we'll only have about ten minutes.'

When the train arrived, the children jumped into the rear coach and locked themselves in the lavatories.

'There's no plug for the wash basin,' said Helen.

'Screw up a paper towel and shove it in,' said Roland.

There was very little soap. Helen and Roland washed themselves frantically, using the towels to scrape away the mud. But although the paper was harsh to the skin, it had no strength. It rolled into shreds, covering everything with pellets of sogginess.

The electric train picked up speed, and the children

were thrown about between the narrow walls. They collided with each other and the wash basin, which slopped water over them at every jolt. There was hardly room to share the mirror, and they were quickly knee-deep in wet paper towels.

In the ten minutes all they managed was to accentuate their wildness. The few patches of skin threw into contrast the mud and plaster.

The children inspected each other under the lamp at the bottom of the station approach. Their house was only fifty yards up the road.

'We've made things worse,' said David. 'We need about six baths each.'

'Do you think we could all sneak into the bathroom without being nabbed?' said Roland.

'We'll try,' said Nicholas. 'But there's going to be a row anyway. We can't hide our clothes.'

'Let's hope the key's not been taken out of the shed yet,' said David.

A spare key to the house was always kept on a ledge above the door inside the coal shed. It was still there. The children crept round to the sittingroom window and listened.

'The TV's on,' said David. 'One of Dad's Westerns.'

'Good: plenty of noise.'

'After me,' said Nicholas. 'And I'll murder anyone who coughs.'

He slid the key into the lock, and waited until there was the cover of gunfire before opening the door. A damp, carbolic, air met them in the hall. Nicholas felt for the light switch and eased it on.

The hall floor and the stairs were carpeted with newspapers. All the furniture was gone, and the shade from the light.

Nicholas closed the door, and led the way. They were

just on the stairs when they heard their mother call, 'Is that you, Nick?'

'It was the switch!' said David. 'It always makes the picture jump.'

'Keep moving,' said Nicholas: then, louder, 'Yes: we're back!'

But it was hopeless. The sittingroom door opened, and there stood Mrs Watson, and behind her a thousand redskins bit the dust.

8. The Deep End

Nicholas ought to have had more sense at his age. What was he thinking of to let everyone get into this state? Didn't he realise that all the clothes were packed? Their mother had quite enough to do without this. Couldn't they be trusted to behave properly when they were out by themselves? And surely there were better ways of spending the time than acting like hooligans in the slums.

The television set was in a bare room among the packing cases. Its own cardboard box was waiting open next to it on the floor. The sound had been turned down at the beginning of the row, which was accompanied as a result by a silent counterpoint of gun battle and cavalry charge. And although the picture was badly distorted, even in the worst moments of the telling off everybody's eyes kept sliding round to the screen.

'And what's that rubbish?' said Mrs Watson.

'Some – things we found,' said Roland.

'And you brought them back? Good heavens, child, what will you do next? Take them outside at once: you don't know where they've been.'

The children escaped to the bathroom while their mother unpacked the cases to find them a change of clothes.

Cleaning was a lot easier than it had been on the train, but the lime in the plaster set hard when they tried to wash their hair.

'Where've you put the Treasures?' said Helen.

'In the shed,' said Roland.

'How are we going to stow them in the furniture van tomorrow?'

'We're not.'

'But we can't leave them!'

'Of course not,' said Roland. 'But the house is going to be empty for at least a month, so we'll hide the Treasures here, and when we've found somewhere safe for them at the new house we'll come back and collect them.'

'Where'll we hide them, though?' said Helen.

'Through the hatch in our room,' said Nicholas.

'Yes,' said David. 'No one'll look there.'

In the wall of the boys' attic there was a door about a foot square, leading into the space between the ceiling joists and the roof. It was too small for an adult to climb through without having a good reason.

'And when Mum's cooled down, perhaps we can tell her about it: or at least ask her to let us keep the Treasures in the house,' said Roland. 'They'll be all right if we clean them up a bit.'

'I've not much hopes of that,' said Nicholas. 'You can't blame Mum for going off at the deep end tonight, and she won't forget it in a hurry. And what are you going to tell her? And who's going to try? If we say, "Mum, we went into an old church and came out in a different place on the other side and these are really four valuable Treasures," what'll happen? You know how hot she is on the truth.'

'But it is the truth,' said Roland.

'And would you believe it if it hadn't happened to you?'

'Yes – if it was somebody I trusted,' said Roland.

'Well, perhaps you would,' said Nicholas. 'But normal people wouldn't.'

'Could we say they're for something one of us is doing at school?' said Helen.

'But it wouldn't be the truth.'

'Oh, Nick!'

'Have you ever tried lying to Mum?' said Nicholas.

'Then what can we do?'

'I don't know,' said Nicholas. 'We've got to manage it by ourselves. No one can help us.'

Among the confusion of the next morning it was easy for the children to hide the Treasures behind the bedroom wall. Roland squeezed through the hatch and laid them out of sight between two joists.

At last the tailboard of the furniture van was fastened,

and the children went on ahead in the car with their parents.

The new house was only about six miles away. Mrs Watson spoke of it as a country cottage, which it may have been a hundred years earlier, but now it stood in a suburban road, and its front door, with the porch, opened on to the footpath.

It was a brick cottage with four rooms and a lean-to kitchen, but Mr Watson had had a bathroom and an extra bedroom built over the kitchen. The old black-leaded grates had been scrapped and replaced with yellow tiles, except for the one in the sittingroom, which Mr Watson had made himself in rustic brick.

Mrs Watson had searched antique shops for horse brasses to hang on the walls, and she had also found three samplers, two coach lamps, and a framed map of the county, hand coloured, and dated 1622.

The cottage was convenient for the station, so that Mr Watson could travel to work in Manchester, yet being in an outer suburb there were fields half a mile away. It was a much smaller house than the one they were leaving, but Mrs Watson said that it was worth the sacrifice for the children to be able to grow up in the country.

The first thing Roland saw when the car turned into the road was the porch.

For an instant he felt that something would happen. The porch was out of place here now: it belonged to Elidor. His vision of it against the Mound had been so clear that the actual porch was a faded likeness by comparison. But suppose when they opened the door there was a passage beyond, lit by a dead light . . .

'Here we are,' said Mr Watson. 'Welcome home, everybody.'

There were newspapers on the floor, but the carbolic smell was going.

They set up base next to the kitchen – in the diningroom, according to Mrs Watson, but the children called it the middle room. The stairs went up one wall, and under them was the larder.

The furniture was unloaded into the sittingroom, which opened by way of the porch straight on to the footpath, without any hall.

By evening it was possible to eat off a table, to watch television, and to sleep.

The children went to bed early. The stairs came through the floor of the boys' room, so they all sat in Helen's, which, being newly built, had a well-fitting door.

'We'd better decide what we can do to keep the Treasures safe,' said Roland.

'Drop them in a lead box and bury them,' said Nicholas.

'We must be able to put our hands on them quickly,' said David, 'in case Malebron wants them back at any time.'

'I don't think he will,' said Nicholas. 'We may as well face it at the start. You saw what came out of the forest, and what were climbing over the battlements. He didn't stand a chance.'

'I thought that at first,' said Roland. 'But I think there was one chance. Didn't you notice something about Malebron right at the end? He wasn't really frightened: he was more excited – as if the important thing was to send us through the door.'

'That's just it,' said Helen. 'He didn't care what happened to him as long as the Treasures were safe.'

'I don't know,' said Roland. 'He said that it was Fear coming out of the Mound, and we were making all those things out of it with our imaginations. Well, he was right, because I'd seen some of them before.'

'You would have!' said Nicholas.

'That bird with arms,' said Roland, 'and that thing with its face in the middle of its chest – they're in those pictures in the art hall at my school. You know: where everybody's being shovelled into Hell.'

'And did you see that tall thin thing covered in hair, with a long nose?' said Helen. 'I can remember dreaming about it when I was little, after I'd been frightened by Mum's fox fur.'

'What are you driving at?' said David. 'Do you mean that those things were real only as long as we were there, or scared of them?'

'So once we'd left Elidor they'd all disappear?' said Helen.

'I think so,' said Roland.

'I hope so,' said Nicholas. 'But we'll probably never know.'

'What are we going to do about the Treasures?' said David. 'Should we make a special place for them which we can keep a secret?'

'Better not,' said Roland. 'If we don't have them with us we can't be sure they're safe.'

'It'd be easier to talk Mum round if we had the real sword to show her,' said David, 'and not two bits of stick.'

'But haven't you noticed?' said Roland. 'The Treasures still feel their own shapes when you hold them. They only look like scrap.'

'Oh, I don't know anything about that,' said Nicholas. 'Yours may feel different, but a stone's just a stone when you're humping it around.'

9. Stat

Roland decided to fetch the Treasures at the end of the first week in the cottage. Every Friday he brought his games clothes home from school in a rucksack, and there would be plenty of room for the cup and the stone, while he could manage the other Treasures easily.

It was left to Roland because he was the only one to go to school by train. He would get off at the station for the old house, collect the Treasures, and catch the next train home.

It felt strange to walk down from the platform with the usual travellers – other schoolchildren, and businessmen old and rich enough to leave their offices at half past three – to walk down the steps, and then to see not the hall light shining through the stained glass of the front door, but a 'For Sale' board behind the hedge, and the windows blank.

When Roland unlatched the gate he realised how much of his life had not moved with him to the cottage. The unique sounds of a house: the noise of that gate, of his feet on that path. Wherever he went he would never take those with him. And yet already there was something different about the house, even after a week. Roland felt it as a kind of awkwardness, almost uneasiness, in his being there, and as he reached the door this suddenly became so strong that the hair on the back of his neck tingled, and his palms were cramped with pins and needles.

It was a sensation so close to fear, and yet Roland was not afraid – then the door opened in front of him as he put the key in the lock.

E.   C

There was a man standing in the shadowy hall.

'What are you on, son?' said the man in a hard, flat, Manchester voice.

'Noth – nothing,' said Roland.

The man was wearing overalls and carried some electrical equipment. Once Roland saw this he was reassured.

'I used to live here. We moved last week, and I've come back to pick up a few things.'

'Such as?'

'Oh, just some bits and pieces.'

'You're not one of these here radio enthusiasts, by any chance?' said the man. 'A little knowledge is a dangerous thing, you know. You could do yourself a mischief.'

'Oh, no,' said Roland. 'My brother's keen, and I've another brother with a transistor set, but I'm no good at that sort of thing.'

'Ay,' said the man. 'There's summat peculiar going on here: there is that.'

'What do you mean?' said Roland.

'Well,' said the man, 'all this week we've had nowt but complaints at the post office from the streets round here about radio and TV interference, and a lot more besides – a proper deluge. So me and me mate comes out in our detector van this afternoon, and there's no two chances about the signal we're getting from this house. There's summat here jamming every frequency we've got and a few more on top, I'd reckon.'

'But the electricity's switched off at the meter,' said Roland.

'I know it is,' said the engineer. 'I had to go to the house agent's for a key, and I've checked mains and wiring. No, it's summat like a generator going full belt – and then some.'

'Can't you tell which room it's in?' said Roland.

'Not a chance. It's too strong. Every needle's peaking high enough to kench itself as soon as we switch on. We'll have to come in the morning and try again. It may just be a freak, though I doubt it.'

He looked back up the stairs.

'And I'll tell you another thing. This house is full of stat.'

'What?'

'Stat – static electricity. And I'll tell you summat else. I can't earth it! What do you say to that?'

'Er – oh, yes?' said Roland.

'Eh? I can't earth it!' said the engineer. 'What?'

'Gosh,' said Roland, since the man persisted in demanding an answer.

'I've not seen owt like it: I have not. It's a right bobby-dazzler.'

The GPO van drove off into the dusk, leaving Roland in the hall. The engineer had warned him not to switch the electricity on, just in case there was a fault that he had not been able to find. But Roland had never intended to make the visit obvious, and he had brought a torch with him.

The air inside the house was so dry that it rustled as he moved. A blue spark cracked between his hand and the banisters when he climbed the stairs, and it felt as though all his hair was on end. Every time he touched anything sparks flashed.

It must be the electricity he was talking about, thought Roland.

He went up to the attic. Roland's lips and mouth pricked with the metallic sweetness of the air. But he reasoned that perhaps this was because he was at the top of the house. He knelt down to open the hatch.

There was a strong smell of ozone in the space under the roof. The Treasures were as he had left them. Roland squirmed through the hatch and went sideways over the joists to avoid the ceiling plaster in between.

The fine dust that lay over everything did not rise when he disturbed it. It was so charged with the static electricity that it clung like fur. Roland felt that he was crawling on an animal.

He worked the Treasures from joist to joist, put them through into the room, and dragged himself after them. He wrapped the stone in his football shirt, and the cup in a towel: then he turned to close the hatch. But there were the shadows of two men in the torchlight on the attic wall.

After the first pulse of horror Roland did not move. He saw every detail of plaster on the wall: he heard every sound in the house and in the road outside. He did not breathe: his mind raced so that every second was ten.

The shadows were not anybody in the room. It was too small and bare for anybody to be in it unseen. And they would have to be between the torch and the wall to make shadows.

This was my bedroom. There's nothing to be frightened of here. They're marks on the wall. Damp patches because the house is empty.

He went closer. They remained the same size. Flat shadows on the wall: motionless, sharp, and black.

It's an optical illusion. I'll shut my eyes and count ten. Or it's all that static electricity. It's a freak, like the man said.

Roland shut his eyes, but he could still see the two figures, reversed like a negative image, yellow against the black screen of his eyelids. He opened his eyes: black on yellow. Closed them: yellow on black: but just as clear. He shook his head, and the men vanished, and then appeared. He turned his head slowly to one side: and back.

He could see the shadows with his eyes closed only when he was facing the wall.

Roland opened his eyes and switched off the torch. In the darkness of the attic the yellow shadows were full size. The air was alive with tiny sparks, and they were thickest round the outline of the shadows, like iron filings clustering about a magnet.

Now the force in the room seemed to hold Roland's head locked in one position so that he could not look away. A numbness was spreading into his limbs, and in his mind and all around him he felt or heard a noise, high, whining, powerful, and the sparks merged into blue flame along the edges of the two shapes.

He willed his hands to switch on the torch, but the flame still showed even in the light, and the blackness of the shadows was more solid than the wall itself. The shadows were becoming independent of the wall, cut loose by the blue flame. They stood both in front of the wall and behind it. They were becoming not shadows, but black holes in the air: holes in space.

Roland felt that if he watched a moment longer

something irrevocable would happen, and that by watching he would be the cause.

He threw himself backwards from the attic and leapt down the stairs. Cold fire blazed round him from the air. He cleared the last six steps to the hall, sensing the whole weight of the house poised over his head. He opened the front door and ran on to the path without looking back. Behind him the door slammed shut on the silent, empty rooms.

10. Choke

Of course it seemed different once he was on the train.

In the brightly lit compartment, and among other people, he realised that there could be a normal explanation for everything. He knew that static electricity could produce strange effects, and the engineer had said there was a lot of it in the house. He had frightened himself before by staring at something quite ordinary in a poor light. 'Come off it, Roland. You're always imagining things.' That was a family joke.

When he reached home Roland put the Treasures on a high shelf in the garage, where they would be unnoticed until they could be hidden in the loft over the bathroom.

By now most of his fright had dropped away. He left the garage, crossed to the house, and shut the kitchen door behind him, all rather quickly, but already the impression of what he had seen was becoming very confused. The shadows were not so clearly shadows; they could have been faults in the wall plaster shown up by the torchlight, or an effect of the dust and the static electricity: somehow.

Friday was the best day of the week. After tea, homework could wait: the first cloud would not appear before Sunday morning. A whole evening lay ahead to be enjoyed.

The children washed up while their mother arranged sandwiches and cake on a trolley for supper. Mr Watson went out in the car to buy a box of chocolates to celebrate their first week in the cottage, and then he brought in coal and stoked the fire.

'Did you get them?' said David to Roland.

'Yes, they're in the garage.'

'What is it on TV tonight, Frank?' said Mrs Watson from the sittingroom.

'I'm just looking, dear,' Mr Watson answered.

'Do you know anything about static electricity?' said Roland.

'A bit,' said David.

'There was an engineer from the post office at the house. He said there'd been complaints. He said the house was full of static electricity, and –'

'It's the circus; then a play; and then ice skating,' said Mr Watson.

'Oh, good! Hurry up, children! The circus is on in a few minutes. And there's a play, and ice skating.'

'– and he said there must be a generator –'

'Right, Mum!' said David. 'Coming! A generator wouldn't give static.'

'But there were sparks everywhere: little blue ones.'

'Never mind,' said Nicholas. 'Leave it. Dad's just switched on.'

The family settled down by the fire. The box of chocolates was passed round; Mrs Watson sited her footstool; Mr Watson polished his glasses with a special cloth impregnated with silicones; they all sat in expectation.

The first thing that happened was that as the television set warmed up it gave out an electronic howl, which climbed the scale until it was like a knife driven through the teeth, and then sank to a scream.

'It's a tuning note,' said Mrs Watson.

'Doesn't sound like it to me,' said David.

'Turn it down a bit, Frank, till it's warmed up,' said Mrs Watson. 'It'll be all right.'

The scream died, and broke into a staccato cough.

'That's not a tuning note,' said David.

The television set blinked, and for a second they glimpsed the head and shoulders of an announcer, and then it looked as if a motor cycle had ridden over his face, leaving the tread marks on the screen and dragging his nose and ears sideways out of the picture.

'It's the Contrast, Frank.'

Mr Watson heaved himself from his chair and began to turn the controls. He was too near to see if he was doing any good. It seemed to be raining in the studio.

'That's better,' said Mrs Watson. 'No! You've gone too far. Back. Oh, that's no good. Try the other way.'

The screen became alternately a dazzling silver and a blackness shot through with meteorites.

'Let me have a go, Dad,' said David.

'Don't interfere,' said Mrs Watson. 'Your father

knows what he's doing. Now. There. There, that's
better.'

It was still raining, but they could tell that some
horses were galloping round a circus ring.

Mr Watson went back to his chair. At that moment
the picture began to float upwards. It was followed by
another. A leisured string of pictures: plop; plop;
plop.

'Your Vertical Hold's gone,' said David.

Mr Watson tramped across the room, and turned
another knob with gentle fury. The pictures slowed. Mr
Watson was breathing through his moustache. The
picture stopped – half out of frame: a black band through
the middle of the screen: above, were galloping hoofs,
below, horses' heads and nodding plumes.

'Ease it up,' said Mrs Watson. 'It's coming – it's
coming. Too much!'

The pictures shot into a fuzz. Mr Watson spun the
knob in both directions, but it had no effect. He turned
all the controls separately and together. He switched
the set off and on again several times. He tried other
channels. Nothing worked.

'Oh, leave it off,' said Mrs Watson. 'It would happen
on Friday.'

'Never mind,' said Mr Watson. 'I'll phone the shop
first thing in the morning.'

'That's not now, is it? What are we going to do?'

'There's tonight's paper, dear, if you'd like to look at
that –'

'Oh, very well. – Thank you.'

Mrs Watson took the evening paper, and made a
point of reading it. Every minute or so she would turn
the pages fretfully, and hit them into shape, as if they
were responsible for the television breakdown.

Mr Watson sat in his chair, gazing at the fire.

David and Roland brought themselves books from upstairs.

Nicholas started to glance through a pile of magazines.

Helen doodled on the cover of one of the magazines, giving a film star a moustache, beard, and glasses.

'Isn't it quiet?' she said.

'I'm going to listen to my transistor,' said Nicholas.

'That's a good idea,' said Mrs Watson. 'Fetch it down, Nick. It'll be nice to have some music if we're reading.'

'I think I'll just try the TV again,' said Mr Watson. 'You never know.'

'Don't,' said Mrs Watson. 'It'll only make you bad tempered. We'll listen to the wireless, and then I'll bring the supper. I shan't be sorry to have an early bed tonight. It's been a tiring week.'

'Have you messed up my transistor?' said Nicholas from the doorway. He was looking at David, and his face was hot.

'Why should I want to touch your puny transistor when I've built a real wireless of my own?' said David.

'Someone has,' said Nicholas. 'Is it either of you two?'

'Not me,' said Roland. 'What's wrong with it?'

'You listen,' said Nicholas, and he pushed the button of his portable radio. A whooping noise rose and fell against a background of atmospheric crackle that drowned any broadcast. 'It's the same on all stations. It was OK this morning, so who's wrecked it?'

'Wait a minute,' said David. He put down his book and ran upstairs.

'I promise we've not touched your wireless,' said Helen.

'No one's been in your room all day, Nick,' said Mrs Watson.

'That's another wash-out, then,' said Nicholas. He flopped into the chair and snatched open a magazine.

'My radio's conked, too!' David called. 'It must be a magnetic storm.'

'Would it stop the TV?' said Mrs Watson.

'No,' said David. 'That doesn't work the same way.'

Nobody could sit still for long. It was so unnatural for the room to be quiet: there was a tension in the silence, as if a clock had stopped.

Mr Watson thumbed the pages of a gardening catalogue. He whistled a tune to himself, but it wasted away.

Every small movement made someone look up, and every sound was an irritation. Then into this silence there broke the noise of a car engine. It hiccupped on one cylinder, hesitated, and the remaining cylinders fired. Mr Watson dropped his catalogue.

'That's our car,' he said.

'Nonsense, Frank.'

'I tell you, it's our car!'

He pulled back the curtain that stopped the draught from the front door, slid the catch, and ran out on to the footpath in his carpet slippers.

'Frank! You'll catch your death!'

They all chased after Mr Watson, and came upon him standing outside the padlocked garage door. Inside the garage the car engine throbbed, about to stall.

'Go and bring a torch and the key, Nick,' said Mr Watson.

The engine picked up again.

'Who can it be? How's he broken in?' said Mrs Watson.

'I don't know, dear,' said Mr Watson. 'It's very funny.'

'Perhaps it's a ghost,' said David.

'David!' said Mrs Watson.

'Oh, no! Do you think it is?' said Helen.

'Of course not. You see what happens when you say stupid things?'

'Sorry, Mum,' said David. 'Only a joke.'

Even so, when Nicholas had brought the key and Mr Watson unlocked the door, everyone felt a creeping of the scalp as the door swung open.

The car stood in a haze of exhaust smoke. Nobody was in the garage. The ignition was switched off, and the key was in Mr Watson's pocket. He sat in the driving seat and frowned at the dashboard.

'Aha,' he said, with an attempt at understanding. 'Ah.'

'What is it, Dad?' said Nicholas.

'I'd not put the choke right back in.'

Mr. Watson stuck his finger against one of the knobs. The engine died.

'There'd be just enough petrol seeping through to fire the engine,' he said. 'Now then, all inside out of the cold! The mystery's solved! Come along!'

'But, Dad,' Roland heard David say as he helped Mr Watson shut the door, 'you'd still need the ignition on to start the motor. Wouldn't you?'

If Mr Watson replied, Roland did not hear him.

The diversion made half an hour pass. It was good to come to the fire from the dark, and they gathered round the hearth, warming their hands, and talking away the uneasiness they had all felt in front of the locked garage.

But the heat of the fire drove them apart to their own little islands in the room. Mr and Mrs Watson faced each other in armchairs. David and Roland, with their shoes off, were competing from behind their books for an unfair share of the sofa. Nicholas sat on a leather pouffe, reading the advice columns in all the magazines. Helen

was drawing heads in profile looking to the left. She could
never draw them looking to the right.

The evening dribbled by.

'Hark,' said Mrs Watson. 'What's that?'

'I can't hear anything,' said Mr Watson.

'It's upstairs.'

The whole family listened.

'Oh, yes,' said Helen. 'It's a – a sort of buzzing.'

'Shut up a minute, then,' said David. 'I can't – oh,
yes –'

'Go and see what it is, Frank,' said Mrs Watson. 'The
immersion heater may not be plugged in properly.'

'Then shall we have supper?' said Mr Watson. 'I
could do with a bite.' His soft, heavy tread creaked on
the stairs.

'Now what's your father up to, I wonder,' said Mrs
Watson after several minutes. 'Has he gone to bed? It'd
be just like him.'

'No,' said Roland. 'He's coming. That noise is louder,
too.'

Mr Watson came downstairs as slowly as he had
climbed. He halted in the doorway of the room: his face
was blank with unbelief. In one hand he held his
electric razor. The razor was working, although in
his other hand Mr Watson held the loose end of the
flex.

'It's my razor,' he said.

'Well, can't you stop it?' said Mrs Watson. 'Can't you
switch it off?'

'There's nothing to switch off. You plug it into the
light.'

'But that's ridiculous, Frank! It's not plugged into
anything. You must be able to switch it off.'

'I can't, dear. It works from the mains.'

'Then what's it doing now?'

'I don't know, dear.'

Mr Watson put the razor on the table. Its vibrations made it turn like the head of a tortoise.

'It was in its case on top of the medicine cupboard. It'd nearly shaken itself off. I had a job to catch it.'

'Dead weird, isn't it?' said Nicholas. 'The power must be coming from somewhere, unless there's a fault.'

'There's no fault in the razor,' said David. 'It's going perfectly!'

'I don't like it,' said Helen. 'It's almost – alive.'

'It's spooky.'

'David!' said Mrs Watson. 'I will not have you putting such thoughts into other people's heads! You know there must always be a perfectly simple explanation for everything that happens. There's obviously something wrong with the razor, and we'll take it back to the shop tomorrow and let a qualified electrician see it.'

'I'll wrap it in a towel and put it away,' said Mr Watson, 'or else it'll get on our nerves. I must say, I wouldn't have thought it.'

'Now we're all up, let's have supper,' said Mrs Watson. 'Will you bring the trolley through, please, Roland, for the cups and saucers? I'll go and put the kettle on.'

'It's still pretty spooky, whatever Mum says,' David muttered.

'Now, David,' said his father.

'Well it is, Dad. You can't run away from it. Things don't start by themselves. You must have something to –'

Mrs Watson's scream interrupted him. They rushed through into the kitchen, and found her staring at the electric food mixer, which was spinning at top speed.

'Switch it off!' cried Mrs Watson.

'It is switched off, Mum,' said Nicholas, and he took

the plug out of the socket, to be certain. The mixer did not falter.

'It – started,' said Mrs Watson. 'I was nowhere near it.'

'Now will you believe me?' said David.

As if to back him up, the drum of the washing machine slowly began to turn behind its glass door.

'It's all right, dear,' said Mr Watson. 'There'll be a fault in the supply. David, go and switch off the mains, and we'll see.'

David pressed a lever on the electricity meter and all the lights in the house went out. But the mixer and the washing machine threshed away in the darkness.

'Very well,' said Mr Watson. 'Put the lights on.'

They ate a poor supper. Mrs Watson was upset, but Mr Watson said that nothing could be done at the moment, and that they should try to have a good night's sleep. It would all be put right in the morning. It was not a fault at the mains, so there was no danger. Nevertheless, he gave himself away by setting up a camp bed for Helen in his room. Now no one would be alone.

At first the boys tried to talk when they were in bed, but their father called to them to go to sleep. So they lay awake through that night, listening to the machinery. At two o'clock in the morning the food mixer burned itself out. But the washing machine rumbled on. The children and their parents stared clear-eyed at the dark.

11. *The Last Spadeful*

'What was that you were chunnering about last night,
Roland, before Dad told you to shut up?' said Nicholas.

'I know what's causing all this,' said Roland. 'It's the
Treasures.'

Mrs Watson was in bed suffering from a headache.
She had put cotton wool in her ears to keep out the noise
of the washing machine. Mr Watson was having trouble
over finding an electrician: either the numbers were en-
gaged, or he became involved in long arguments.

'I don't know how they're doing it,' said Roland, 'but
they are. Malebron said they'd still give light in Elidor
even when they're here, so they must be generating
something.'

'Generators!' said David. 'Yes! They could! Roland,
you've hit it! If Malebron said that, the Treasures must
be giving off energy. And if it's generated over a wide
enough range of frequencies it'll spoil TV and radio
reception – and it'll turn electric motors!'

'Does that mean that as long as I'm looking after a
stone I'll not be able to use my transistor?' said Nicholas.

'It depends what the range is,' said David. 'But probably you won't.'

'It fits what happened when I went to collect them,'
said Roland. 'The GPO van, and all that static.'

'The van makes sense,' said David. 'But generators
generate static electricity. And if the Treasures are
generators–'

'There's a lot of "if" in this,' said Nicholas.

'But we'll have to do something quickly,' said Roland.
'We can't hide the Treasures for long. They'll be found

and taken away from us. There'll be another van looking for them this morning, I bet, unless we can stop the interference they're causing.'

'The only thing to do is to try and screen them,' said David. 'If we put them in a metal box and bury them it should block out most of the interference, if the energy is anything like electricity – and it must be, even in Elidor.'

'That's what I said we should do at the start,' said Nicholas. 'Dig a hole and bury 'em. Well, it's a bit thick if I can't listen to the radio. And anyway, we look so daft carting these things round – you and Roland playing soldiers with bits of iron and wood, and Helen at a doll's tea party, and me – well, what am I doing looking after a lump of stone as if it was the crown jewels?'

'But Malebron trusted us to look after them,' said Roland. 'We can't let him down. And Elidor –'

'You give me the pip sometimes,' said Nicholas. 'You really do. All right: I was as excited as you when it happened. But what is it once you've got used to the idea? Is it any better than our world? It's all mud and dust and rock. It's dead, finished. Malebron said so. And you should think about him a bit more, too. Did he care how we made out as long as he found his Treasures? He sent us trotting off into that Mound one after the other, but he didn't go in himself. What right has he to expect us to spend the rest of our lives like – like broody hens?'

'But you saw him,' said Roland. 'How can you forget him if you've seen him?'

Nicholas shrugged his shoulders. 'Oh, well,' he said. 'Well. Well, I didn't say anything was wrong with him: he was just self-centred.'

'Do stop arguing,' said Helen. 'Honest, Roland, if David's right, then what Nick wants to do is best even if you don't like why he's doing it.'

'Now what's all this noise?' said Mr Watson. The

washing machine had covered his approach. 'You know your mother's got a bad head.'

'Sorry, Dad,' said David. 'Any luck?'

'It's very strange,' said Mr Watson, 'but every single electrician says he's been having calls all night, and no one can promise to come before this afternoon.'

'So it wasn't just us,' said David.

'It's intolerable,' said Mr Watson. 'Your poor mother didn't sleep a wink. I'm going round to the electricity office now to insist that they do something immediately. It can't go on.'

'Can we dig in the garden, please?' said Helen.

'Yes: yes: anything you like,' said Mr Watson, 'as long as you don't disturb your mother. She's dropped off.'

'We'll have to bury the Treasures,' said David as soon as their father had gone. 'If they've been causing all this trouble, the electricity people or the post office will find them. It's the only way, Roland.'

'David and I'll take first go at the digging,' said Nicholas. 'We'll have to make it deep, and Dad won't think much of it if he comes back before we've finished.'

Helen and Roland went upstairs and brought down four polythene bags to hold the Treasures. It was hard to squash all the air out of the bags so that they would take up as little space as possible. Helen fastened the necks with rubber bands, and covered this seal with a lashing of twine. Roland found an old dustbin among the rubbish that had been cleared out of the cottage and was waiting to be removed from the bottom of the garden.

The Treasures looked no different: a stone, a piece of railing, two laths, and a cup. Roland put them into the dustbin and tied the lid down with a length of flex from David's radio spares.

When Helen and Roland climbed into the hole it was

up to their chests. The sides were mottled layers of earth, darkest at the top, growing lighter and sandier towards the bottom, and veined brown with dead roots. Sherds of pottery winked blue and white in the soil.

'Have you noticed?' said Helen. 'Wherever you dig there's always millions of broken plates. It was the same at the other house. People must have been throwing them away for years.'

They were head-deep in almost pure sand, and they could barely lift the spade loads to clear the pile at the edge of the hole.

'You'll do at that,' said David. 'It's the best we can manage in the time. Give us your hand and I'll pull you out.'

'Right,' said Helen. 'Last spadeful coming up – oh!'

She drove the spade into the sand, and it hit something which cracked. Helen knelt and picked out several fragments of earthenware.

'Oh, I think it was a whole jug!' she said. 'And I've smashed it. Look, Roland. Oh, isn't it lovely!'

She wiped a piece with her hand. It was a creamy brown colour, with a blue tinge of lead in the glaze, and there were the head and forelegs of a unicorn lined in dark red.

'Gosh, it must be centuries old,' said Roland.

'I'm going to mend it,' said Helen. 'Oh, what a pity! If only I hadn't broken it! I'd give anything not to have broken it!'

'We'll be copped if you don't hurry up,' said Nicholas.

Helen and Roland were pulled out of the hole, and the dustbin was lowered in. They kicked and shovelled the earth back, and stamped it down.

'There,' said Nicholas.

When they went into the kitchen to clean their hands the washing machine had stopped.

12. The Letterbox

Electricians checked the house, and went away again. Mr Watson made a flower bed on the heap of soil where the Treasures were buried. A year passed.

And all this time Roland avoided using the front door. He felt that he could never trust the door to be the way out of and into the cottage. It became a compulsion, like walking on kerbstones.

Helen mended the jug she had found in the hole. It was a large pitcher, and it had broken into five pieces. She spent hours glueing them together, almost in tears when she thought of what she had done. The pitcher had lain in the ground such a long time, and such a little care would have saved it. Now she was too late, and nothing could make it whole again.

The unicorn reared below the lip, poised at the height and stillness of movement. An instant later, Helen thought, and it would have been gone.

There was no other decoration except for two lines of thick black lettering under the unicorn,

> *Save mayde that is makeles*
> *Noe man with me mell.*

'What does it mean, Dad?' said Nicholas.

'I'm not sure,' said Mr Watson. 'It's some sort of verse – perhaps it's a family motto, something like, you know, that Scottish one, "He gets hurt who meddles with me".'

'What's a makeless maid?' said Roland.

'Well, it's hard to say exactly. I suppose you could find it in the dictionary.'

'You've made a very good job of mending that, Helen,' said Mrs Watson. 'You can't really see the cracks.'

'But I know they're there,' said Helen.

The year passed. It was a dark Sunday afternoon. Helen and Nicholas had gone for a ride on their bicycles: David and Roland were sitting at the table in the middle room, revising the work they had done at school that term. Through the window they could see their mother and father in the garden. Mr Watson was planting some rose bushes.

Roland tried to concentrate on his history book. He had to read twenty pages, and he found that he was more aware of the number of a page than of what was printed on it. Eventually the words became a procession, and his mind drifted from them, first to the tablecloth, and then to the window. He saw that David was drawing patterns in the margin of his notebook.

'Revision's the worst part of the term, isn't it?' said Roland. 'You think you know the stuff, but you don't: and you can't take it in because you've heard it all before and it's gone stale.'

'I can't get used to not having a front garden,' said David. 'Every time someone goes past the house I think they're coming here. And that front door's driving me round the bend.'

'Oh?' said Roland. 'Why?'

'It keeps buzzing,' said David. 'Haven't you noticed? It must be traffic that makes it vibrate. Anyway, what with that, and the footpath right next to the house, you can't think straight, even in here.'

'I've never liked the porch,' said Roland. 'I used it to open the Mound, and ever since it's felt wrong.'

'What?' said David. 'Open what?'

'The Mound,' said Roland. 'In Elidor.'

'Oh, that,' said David.

'What do you mean, "Oh, that"?' said Roland. 'Elidor! Elidor! Elidor! Have you forgotten?'

'OK,' said David. 'We don't want the whole road to hear.'

'Elidor,' said Roland. 'So why can't we talk about it? You and Nick always change the subject.'

'I think you ought to cool down a bit on this Elidor business,' said David.

'You're mad!' said Roland.

'All right,' said David, 'we have been talking about it.'

'I don't remember,' said Roland.

'Nick said you'd only start getting worked up and we'd have a row, so we didn't tell you.'

'Good old Nick!' said Roland. 'He would! Thanks very much!'

'You see?' said David. 'You're shouting already.'

'But you're pretending it doesn't matter,' said Roland. 'Didn't it mean anything to you – Malebron and the Treasures, and that golden castle, and, and – everything?'

'Listen,' said David, 'Nick's not all that dim, although you think he is. A lot of what he says makes sense, even if I don't agree with everything myself.'

'What does he say, then? That there's no such place as Elidor, and we dreamed it?'

'In a way,' said David.

'He's off his head.'

'No, he's gone into it more than any of us,' said David. 'And he's been reading books. He says it could all have been what he calls "mass hallucination", perhaps something to do with shock after the church nearly fell on us. He says it does happen.'

'And I suppose the mud we scraped off was a mass hallucination,' said Roland.

'Yes, I know,' said David. 'But I think he may be right about the Treasures. Try to remember. When the church was shaking all round us we couldn't see what we were doing, and we were falling all over the place, and everything jarred so much we didn't know where we were. That's true, isn't it?'

'I suppose so.'

'Well,' said David, 'even if we were holding the real Treasures they could have been knocked out of our hands and we could have grabbed hold of the other things without noticing.'

'I didn't,' said Roland.

'But it is possible,' said David.

'If you can believe that, you can believe in the Treasures,' said Roland. 'And what about the things that happened next? The television, and Dad's razor, and your theory about generators?'

'Yes, it was a bit rum,' said David. 'But it could have been a coincidence. And anyway it was a long time ago. And nothing's happened since.'

'That's the whole point!' said Roland. 'That's why

we buried them! If we dug them up it'd start all over again.'

'There's not much chance of that,' said David. 'Now that Dad's made his prize flower bed there, it'd be more than anyone's life's worth to touch it.'

David and Roland looked out of the window into the garden. Roland was about to go on with the argument, but what he saw stopped him.

Mr Watson was crouching a few feet away from a rose bush that he had just planted. Others lay nearby, their roots in bags. Very gingerly, and rather like a boxer, Mr Watson sidled towards the flower bed. He stretched out his hand, flinching: nearer: and nearer; then he jumped back as if the bush had bitten him. The children watched him do this twice before they left their work and ran into the garden.

'What's up, Dad?' said David.

By this time Mrs Watson had joined her husband and was peering at the bush.

'It's this Mrs A. R. Barraclough,' said Mr Watson. 'I keep getting a shock from it.'

'A shock?'

'No, not quite, but there's a distinct sound when I try to touch it, and I can feel a tingling in my hand.'

'Your hair's all frizzy, too, Frank,' said Mrs Watson. 'How very interesting: look, David and Roland. There must be thunder about somewhere.' She put her hand near the bush, and they all heard a sharp crack.

'Be careful, dear,' said Mr Watson.

'It's all right, Dad,' said David. 'That's static electricity.'

Roland hurried to different parts of the garden, touching shrubs, trees, walls, fences.

'There's nothing here,' he called. He came back to the

flower bed and put out his hand. Crack. 'It's only this place.' He looked hard at David.

'Run and see if the glass is dropping, Roland,' said Mrs Watson. 'I do hope Helen and Nick aren't going to be caught in a storm.'

Roland went into the house. His face was flushed, and he was breathing quickly.

The barometer hung on the sittingroom wall. The needle was slightly higher than it had been the previous day.

'Coincidence!' said Roland. 'Huh!'

While he was reading the barometer the front door vibrated – a short, resonant buzz, not very loud, but noticeable. He had heard it before on several occasions, but it was only now since David had complained about it that the sound grated on him.

The door buzzed again, a longer note. Roland turned from the barometer, and as he passed the door he heard someone step into the porch. There was no mistaking this. The footpath had its own sound, and so had the porch. The flagstone gave a hard echo between the brick walls. Someone had stepped into the porch.

Without waiting for the knock, Roland drew back the curtain. The upright letterbox in the top of the door was open, and pressed close against it Roland saw an eye.

He snatched the curtain across and held it tightly in place. He heard a slight movement, and the door knob was turned both ways, and the door shifted against the Yale lock. He could hear breathing, too.

'Who is it?' said Roland.

No one answered. The door still buzzed.

Roland dashed out into the garden. 'There's someone trying to get in through the front door!' he shouted.

It was so obvious that Roland was frightened that Mr Watson dropped his spade and hurried round the side of the house to the footpath. Helen and Nicholas were wheeling their bicycles on to the kerb.

'Who's in the porch?' said Mr Watson.

'I didn't notice anybody,' said Nicholas.

The porch was empty, and so was the road.

'Why? What's the matter?'

'Someone looked through the letterbox and tried to open the door,' said Roland. 'Now: about half a minute ago.'

'But they couldn't have,' said Helen. 'We were free-wheeling to see who could get nearest to home without touching the pedals. We were ages coming down the road.'

'Nobody went anywhere near the house,' said Nicholas.

'Yes, they did!' cried Roland. 'I heard them, and when I pulled the curtain there was this eye – staring!'

'Who'd want to do that?' said Nicholas. 'There'd be nothing to see but curtain.'

'Was it you frightening Roland, Nick?' said Mr Watson.

'Me? No!'

'Because if it was, I've told you before I won't stand for it. You're old enough to know better than to play stupid tricks like that.'

'But it wasn't me, Dad!'

'Very well,' said Mr Watson. 'But I don't want it to happen again, that's all.'

'I did see somebody!' said Roland. 'I did!'

'Now come along inside, Roland,' said Mrs Watson. 'You know, you're your own worst enemy.'

'But Mum, I did see somebody!'

'I don't doubt it,' said Mrs Watson. 'But you mustn't let your imagination run away with you. You're too highly strung, that's your trouble. You'll make yourself ill if you're not careful.'

Roland was found to have a temperature of a hundred and one. Mrs Watson gave him aspirin and sent him to bed, cooked him a light tea, and sat with him until he appeared to be calmer.

When the other children went to bed they were told to go quietly so as not to wake Roland. They tip-toed upstairs without switching the light on.

'Come in here, you lot,' said Roland.

13. 'Silent Night'

Next morning the static electricity had dispersed. The rose bed was normal.

At this time of the year it was dark when the children came home, and so the only chance Roland had of inspecting the garden was after breakfast. Monday, Tuesday, Wednesday passed, and nothing happened. He tried to vary his approach so that no one would see what he was doing. He brought in coal, or carried cinders out, or threw scraps for the birds. He noticed that food landing near the bed was always the last to be taken, and the sparrows and starlings never gathered there to fight over a crust as they did in the rest of the garden. A single bird would dart in and snatch the food, and the quarrelling would not begin until the bird was clear of the rose bed.

On Thursday morning Roland was having his breakfast when Mrs Watson threw a piece of burned toast out of the window. The toast fell on the path, and lay untouched. Roland saw one bird fly down from a chimney, but when it was over the garden it braked in the air, shot sideways, and flew back to the chimney, where it sat, ruffling its feathers and wagging its head. A few minutes later it tried again, with the same result. No other birds came near.

As soon as he could Roland went into the garden. There were plenty of birds in the orchard over the fence next door, but they were all silent. Roland crossed the path, and as he came near to the rose bed his hair started to move on his neck, and the palms of his hands tingled.

By smuggling his mackintosh into the last lesson Roland was able to leave school as soon as the bell rang. He cut through the playing field and ran a mile to the station, and so caught the early train, which went half an hour before his usual one. Roland sprawled in the carriage. His shirt was out of his trousers, rumpled in sticky folds on his back. He felt as if he was bursting in the carriage heat: but he would reach home before dark.

The street lamps were on when he walked up the road from the station. He plucked leaves off the hedges as he passed. Ivanhoe, Fern Bank, Strathdene, Rowena, Trelawney: respectable houses bounded by privet, each with its square of grass. Two days ago the first Christmas tree had appeared in a front room window, and now every house had one displayed, and they were all bigger than the first tree.

Whinfield, Eastholme, Glenroy, Orchard Main. What could happen here? thought Roland. Even the toadstools are made of concrete. But it's our house that has the porch . . .

He stopped in front of the porch, smelling the bitter privet leaves rolled between his fingers. The name of the house, carved on a varnished section of log, hung from two chains, by the arch. Screwed into the door was a plaque which said, 'Here live Gwen and Frank Watson', then came a knot of flowers, and underneath, 'with Nicholas, David, Helen, and Roland'. But the porch still did not belong. It makes it worse, thought Roland. They'll know they've found us.

He went into the garden. There was nothing to be felt. Roland put his school books away before going back to the rose bed. He touched the bushes, prodded the soil, walked round the bed. What makes it come? Is it the Treasures? If it is, why isn't it there all the time?

There was hardly any light except for the afterglow of

the sun in the clear sky. The ground was freezing already. And then, in the middle of Roland's casting about, he felt the static electricity as suddenly as if a switch had been pressed.

And when he looked at the rose bed he saw the shadows of two men standing there.

They were motionless, as they had appeared in the attic wall. Flat shadows. But they were not thrown on anything solid, they were shadows on the air.

Roland backed away to the path, and the shadows stayed where they were. He edged round to the side. They narrowed with perspective until he was at right-angles to them, and then they disappeared until he moved past them. They were visible from in front and behind, and Roland could not see through them. And yet they were two-dimensional: they had no depth: looked at from the side, there was not a hair-line of darkness.

Roland went closer to the rose bed. He was both frightened and excited by the shadows.

'Just stay there,' he said. 'Just stay there. They'll have to listen after this. Just stay there till the others come.'

His throat ached, and the ache moved into the neck muscles, sending a sharp pain through his forehead. The air pricked with light: the shadows gleamed like ink. Roland's neck was cramped fast. He remembered how it had been in the attic, how he had watched until it was nearly too late. He was doing something by looking at the shadows, and the whining noise was coming now. He forgot about proving himself right. It was too dangerous. He had to move, while he could.

Roland floundered across the garden towards the house. His knees and the small of his back felt as though they were bubbles of air, and the ground was never where he thought it was.

'Your tea's ready,' Mrs Watson called when she heard Roland in the kitchen.

'Thanks, Mum,' he said.

It was eight o'clock before all the family was ready to watch the television. Mr Watson had settled down about ten minutes earlier, and so when Mrs Watson and the children joined him they were surprised to find that he had not switched the television on.

'Is something wrong, Frank?' said Mrs Watson.

'No. I'm listening to the carol singers. They're the first this year.'

In the distance they could hear uncertain treble voices.

'*Silent Night*,' said Mr Watson. 'My favourite.'

'I heard them three weeks ago,' said Mrs Watson. 'They start earlier every year.'

'I suppose, before long,' said Mr Watson, 'they'll run it in with Guy Fawkes and get all the collecting done at one go.'

'Are we having the telly on, Dad?' said Nicholas.

'In a minute,' said Mr Watson, 'in a minute. Let's be seasonable. It's not every night of the year we can hear carols, and we'll have to pay for them, so let's have our money's worth. They sound as though they're outside Mrs Spilsbury's. We should get them at the next move.'

But as he said this, they heard the scuffle of feet in the porch.

'Oh, really,' said Mr Watson. 'Already? It's a bit much to expect to be paid for something we can't hear. Go away! We want *Silent Night* outside the window before you have a penny!' He winked at the others. 'I'll complain to your union!'

There was a further scuffle, and the doorknob rattled.

'Young scamps,' said Mr Watson. 'They might have the decency to knock. Go away! Off with you!'

A pause. Then they heard footsteps on the pavement, and a whispered muttering, and then, still whispered, 'Ready? One, two, three,' and several voices in different keys began to sing *Away in a Manger*. Before they reached the end of the first line there was a polite knock at the door. 'That's more like it,' said Mr Watson, and opened the door.

'Merry Christmas,' said the small boy in the porch. He brandished a money box. 'And a Happy New Year.'

'Now why couldn't you do it properly the first time?' said Mr Watson. 'There was no need to rattle the door like that. And I did ask for *Silent Night*.'

The boy gaped at him.

'What d'you mean, mister? We've been up the road. No one rattled your door.'

'Come now, come,' said Mr Watson. 'I distinctly heard you larking about in my porch.'

'We never –'

'Thank you!' said Mr Watson.

'We didn't –'

'I said thank you. Now listen: all I'm asking is that you sing what I requested – *Silent Night* – and that you refrain from rattling my door. That's reasonable, isn't it?'

'No one rattled your door, mister,' said the boy. 'We weren't anywhere near your door.'

14. The High Places

Roland said nothing about the shadows. When the other children had come home he had not had the courage to go outside again. He realised, too, that nothing less than the shadows themselves would convince Nicholas, and next morning and all Saturday there was no static charge in the garden.

'I wish you'd have a look at that front door, Frank,' said Mrs Watson at tea on Saturday. 'It judders every time a car goes past. It's the kind of noise that sets my teeth on edge: I could hardly sew for it this afternoon. It's become much worse lately.'

'Very good, dear,' said Mr Watson. 'I'll see what can be done in the morning. It may need a touch of the screwdriver.'

'And I wish you had paid those boys the other night, instead of preaching at them. They've been in and out of that porch all day. It's their way of getting their own back, I suppose.'

'I explained at the time that it was a matter of principle,' said Mr Watson. 'But what have they done now?'

'Oh, they've been dragging their feet, turning the doorknob, flapping the letterbox – that sort of thing.'

'Didn't you stop them?' said Mr Watson.

'They're much too quick. They're off and out of sight the moment they hear the curtain rings move. I gave it up after the second time. They'll soon tire of it when they see we're not to be drawn.'

'Or they'll be provoked to worse mischief,' said Mr Watson. 'My mother was once nearly frightened to death when some louts dropped a rip-rap through her letter-box. It could have set the house on fire, too. Oh, no: we must put a firm stop to it.'

'Listen,' said Nicholas. 'They're at it again. Shall David and I nip out and clobber them?'

'Certainly not,' said Mr Watson. 'I mean to deal with this once and for all. I'm going to catch them from behind. You just go on talking normally.'

'Don't do anything silly, Frank,' said Mrs Watson.

Mr Watson let himself out by the back door. The children and their mother listened to the shuffling that was going on in the porch.

'Sounds as though there's quite a few of them,' said David. 'I wonder if Dad will be all right.'

'Don't be daft,' said Nicholas. 'That kid who was collecting was only eight or nine. I still think we should clobber them. Dad'll lay the law down, but he won't do anything else, except ask their names and addresses. And who'd be mug enough to give him real ones?'

The back door opened, and Mr Watson stamped in.

'Too late!' he said. 'Not a soul in sight.'

'We heard them all the time you were out, Frank,' said Mrs Watson. 'They've never stopped. Are you sure you went?'

'My dear Gwen,' said Mr Watson, 'the street lamp across the road shines right into the porch. They're hiding in gateways, but I'm not playing their game for them.'

'They are not hiding, Frank. You didn't listen to what I said. They were in the porch all the time, and they are there now.'

'Eh? What? Good heavens!'

The letterbox snapped shut.

'But this is preposterous!'

Mr Watson was pale with indignation.

'We'll soon deal with that, though! If I open the door when they're not expecting it, I'll trap them against the porch. Then we'll see who's being so funny.'

'No, Dad!' said Roland. 'Don't. Please don't.'

Mr Watson frowned Roland to silence, and put his hand on the catch, taking care not to move the brass rings on the curtain. The doorknob turned. Mr Watson threw the door open.

'Got you!'

'Dad! No!'

Roland tried to reach his father to pull him away, but he became entangled in the curtain. Mr Watson was thrusting the door hard against the inside wall of the porch.

'Now then,' he said. 'Now then.'

But as he eased the pressure, the heavy oak door scooped him off his feet and slammed him back into the room. The door crashed shut, and Mr Watson fell over Roland, tearing the curtain down on top of them both.

Nicholas pushed forward. 'No. Don't go,' said Mrs Watson. There had been something brutal in the speed with which the door had moved. 'Nick.'

They dragged the curtain from Mr Watson. He was sitting dazed on the floor, and one eye was beginning to close. His nose was bleeding.

'Hooligans!' he said. 'Arrant hooligans!'

'You go looking for trouble,' said Mrs Watson when she bathed his eye. 'For all you know it could be one of those teenage gangs off the overspill.'

'You said it was the carol singers.'

'I know I did, but it wasn't, was it? Eight-year-olds wouldn't have done this, would they? Roland, come away from that window. You'll egg them on to something else if they're still hanging around. Ignore them, and they soon lose interest.'

Roland watched the poplar branches curling like tentacles round the street lamp. The road glistened. But he knew that when he had stood next to his father at the door, all beyond the porch had been in darkness, except for the glow of a log fire burning near by.

It was three in the morning when Roland went downstairs. Coals tinkled in the grate, and the clock raced with the double note that Roland never heard in daylight. The front door vibrated, although the only traffic was the long-distance lorries on the main road a quarter of a mile away.

He knew that it was up to him to do something. After this there would be more than curiosity.

He listened at the curtain. He had switched off the pencil torch and clipped it in his pyjama pocket. There was no sound of movement or breathing in the porch, and so Roland eased himself into the space between the curtain and the door. Still no sound, apart from the quiet jarring of the wood. The air smelled of curtain, and a thin draught slipped round him: the coconut matting needled his feet. Roland braced himself on to his toes and looked with one eye through a gap between the letterbox frame and its hinge.

Now that the room was dark Roland could see quite well in the shadow-light of Elidor.

It was nowhere that he recognised. In his narrow angle of vision there was nothing but mountains: peaks, crags, ice, and black rock stabbed upwards. The porch seemed to be at the top of a cliff, or a knife-backed ridge. Roland had the sensation of a sheer drop behind him in the room. Down the mountainside in front lay a camp of tents, and there was a hunting party winding from it up a track that passed the door. The men rode stags and carried lances, and some had bows across their backs. Wolfhounds ran before them. Close to the porch there was a bivouac in the shelter of a rock. Here the fire Roland had glimpsed burned pale and colourless, and next to it squatted a man holding a spear.

A hound sniffed at the porch, but was called off sharply. The riders looked at the door as they went by. One of them spoke to the man at the fire, who was now standing, He shook his head and pointed with the spear down to the camp.

At this moment the door stopped vibrating, and the scene vanished, and Roland was squinting out at his own night, and all he could hear was the lorries.

He lowered his heels. The man had been a sentry, guarding the porch. They had found it. They knew it was a way through. They would come when they were ready. It's my fault, thought Roland. I made it. What can I do?

The door buzzed again. He lifted himself up.

Although only a few seconds had passed, it must have been longer in Elidor. The fire was bigger, and there was a different sentry. The new man was walking up and down to keep warm.

It must be freezing, thought Roland. And why do they need such a huge camp? They can't live up here all the time: there's nothing but rock and ice, thousands of feet high. – High. – A high place. – High places. – 'Who walks in the High Places'. Findhorn. That's it: the Song of Findhorn. Malebron was going to look. He said there were mountains. Then they're looking, too!

It was impossible that this could be Malebron's camp. These men had his nobility, his bearing, his dress, but only Malebron had had the golden light about him. Their beauty was the beauty of steel, every line of them cut hard as an engraving.

Oh, what can I do? thought Roland.

The sentry halted, and stared at the letterbox, as if he had heard Roland speak. Then he came towards the door.

Roland slid down as far as he could. He heard the familiar footsteps in the porch, and a hand pushed the letterbox open: the knob was turned; the door moved against the lock: scuffle: and silence. When Roland dared to look the sentry was bending over the fire and stirring food in a pot.

It's my fault. I made it. I made it. The answer stopped him.

I must unmake it.

Roland fixed his eye on the porch. Go away. Disappear. Scram. Go on. The porch did not hear. Roland tried to will it away, to think of nothing, but he could not imagine 'nothing': it had no shape to build in his mind. He felt as weak as if he was pushing the bricks with his hands.

The sentry was restless and kept walking over to the door.

Think, Roland told himself. Think. How does a house fall? You don't just shove it over. The church. What happened first? It was the mortar between the bricks: running out. That's it. Bricks can't stay up without mortar.

He closed his eyes and pictured the arch in his mind. When it was fixed there he concentrated on the joints of the brickwork. Grey mortar. Loose. Dry. Crumbling. Oh, come on. Come on.

Roland heard a sound, a whisper like rain on leaves. He heard it again. A thin dust was settling in the porch. Come on, you porch! You're not all real. You're an echo: not all solid. Come on, you echo!

The mortar grew to a trickle. He dared to open his eyes, and although the dust-fall slackened it did not stop. He forced his mind like a drill between the bricks of the porch in Elidor.

The sentry yelled, but Roland broke his concentration only long enough to see that the man had noticed what was happening, and was running to the camp.

Come on! Break! Come on! More! A brick fell, and another, and a crack went up to the roof. That's it! He picked at the gap, heaving, tearing. It was easier. The bricks dropped. If he could undermine the roof, the weight of the stone tiles would pull the whole thing down. But he was labouring now with the cutting edge of his mind dulled, and every stroke was taking more energy to drive home. Men were hurrying from the camp. He sobbed and groaned and hit unaimed blows at the porch with all his will.

The men carried two-handed axes, and the first to reach the door swung his axe down into the wood. The house boomed like a drum. The axe was wrenched out, and up, and down it smashed again. Roland gathered his energy and made one blind lunge. Everything of him poured out, and after that there was nothing: and into this nothing the porch began to fall.

A third time the axe struck, but the blade was muffled, and the fourth made no sound at all. The men shouted in silence, and the porch grew dim. Beyond the peaks of the mountains two beams of yellow light flashed in the sky, and behind the sky was a bloom of darkness. The shadow of another porch covered the bricks, close as a skin, but whole where the arch was broken. The man with the axe hewed the door, yet could not touch it, and he jumped clear as the roof and walls crashed towards him, and Elidor drowned in the headlights of a car that was turning off the main road. The twin yellow beams flickered through the poplar trees, and glanced from the wall of the porch. Roland sagged against the door. The wood was like ice on his brow.

15. Planchette

The telephone rang while Mr Watson was having breakfast.

'That was the Brodies,' he said when he came back to the table. 'They're giving a party for their two on the twenty-ninth, and ours are invited. There'll be a card in the post, but John Brodie wanted to know now so that the date can be fixed. It'll be your night out,' he said to the children, 'to make up for when your mother and I go to the Greenwoods' New Year dance.'

'I'm still not sure about that,' said Mrs Watson. 'They're young to be left.'

'They're plenty old enough to look after themselves,' said Mr Watson. 'Aren't you?'

'But do we have to go to this party?' said Nicholas.

'Of course,' said Mrs Watson. 'It'll be great fun. And the Brodies are such nice people. We ought to see more of them.'

'But we don't know the kids,' said Nicholas. 'It sounds deadly. I can't stand pass-the-parcel.'

'We've accepted now,' said Mr Watson. 'And it lasts till eleven-thirty, so I think you'll find it's quite a grown-up party.'

'Oh, heck,' said Nicholas.

'I must remember to put them on the Christmas card list,' said Mrs Watson.

David came in from outside.

'Dad! Have you seen the front door? It isn't half a mess!'

There were three gashes in the door. Two of them were cut an inch into the oak, but the third was more of a dent, as if it had been made with less force than the others.

'I thought I heard banging in the night,' said Mrs Watson, 'but I must have turned over again.'

'But this is vandalism!' said Mr Watson. 'We're being persecuted. It's – it's intolerable. Really, the lengths they'll go to just to vent their spite. Why, this must have been done with an axe!'

'That's what you must expect when you have overspill in a decent area,' said Mrs Watson. 'They shouldn't be allowed to build out in the country. People aren't going to change when they move from the city. And goodness knows what it will do to property values.'

'It's sheer vandalism,' said Mr Watson.

But later in the day he filled the gashes with a wood compound, and tightened the hinges and the door catch, which seemed to cure the vibrations.

'I thought a touch of the screwdriver would do the trick,' he said.

The party loomed. The Brodies lived in a big house that had stood by itself among fields but was now surrounded by the local council's new estate. Both the children went to boarding school.

'It's going to be wet,' said Nicholas as they set out on the night.

'Oh, I don't think so,' said Mr Watson. 'Hard frost. Clear sky. It'll stay like this for a couple of days at least. The glass is very steady.'

'I meant the party,' said Nicholas.

Jennifer and Robert Brodie met the Watsons formally on the doorstep. There were about a dozen other guests, and they drank fruit cup. They played games, 'to break the ice'. These involved pushing a matchbox from nose to nose, and mixing the girls' shoes up and then having to find the owners.

Then they danced to gramophone records. But Helen was the only one of the four who could dance. Nicholas had had two lessons, which made him more wretched than anybody. There were Excuse-me Dances, and Novelty Dances, and Forfeit Dances. Those without a partner had to dance with a mop.

At nine o'clock they went in to supper. There was a game with name-cards to decide who sat where, but Nicholas cheated so that the Watsons were together and at the far end of the table.

'Isn't it smashing!' said Helen.

'Two and a half hours more,' said David.

'Can't we go now?' said Roland.

But the food was good. The Brodie children called their father Jo-jo, and he told funny stories all the time. Then everybody started to pull crackers. Roland pulled his with Helen. He unrolled the paper hat, and read the motto, and shook the cracker to see if it was empty. Something dropped on to the table.

'What's up, Roland?' said David. 'Are you feeling sick?'

'What have you got?' said Roland.

'A hat; and a motto; same as you.'

'What else?'

'Only one of those useless bits of junk you always have in crackers.'

'What is it?'

'A tie clip, or something: a kind of sword made of pink plastic. It says "Hong Kong" on the back.'

'I've got a spear,' said Roland.

'Mine's a little plastic goblet,' said Helen.

'What have you got, Nick?' said Roland.

'Please, Roland!' said Helen. 'Please don't go on!'

'What's inside your cracker?' said Roland.

'Calm down,' said Nicholas. 'You'll have them thinking you've gone barmy.'

'Tell me what's in that cracker besides the hat and the motto!'

'Oh, that,' said Nicholas. 'A pink brick. Do you want it?'

'A brick? You mean a stone!'

'Oh, good grief, Roland! Not again! Anyway, it's a dice. And it's a pretty poor one, too. The spots aren't coloured.'

'It's shaped like a stone; it could be made of stone even if it is a dice,' said Roland.

'Well it isn't, it's made of plastic, and so's everything else.'

'It's pushing things a bit,' said David. 'Or are you saying Malebron's sending us souvenirs from Hong Kong?'

'I don't know what I'm saying –'

'That's true,' said Nicholas.

'– but it's not a coincidence.'

'Of course it's a coincidence,' said Nicholas.

'Then if it is,' said Roland, 'it coincides with something. You don't have a coincidence on its own. And what it coincides with is the Treasures. It makes them more real.'

David crossed and uncrossed his eyes.

'You can't laugh them off now!' said Roland. 'Everything's linked. Malebron said so. Even if these are bits of a cracker, they're part of something else, and you can't get away from it.'

'Oh, do belt up,' said Nicholas.

'Are we all happy down this end of the table?' said Mr Brodie, appearing behind David's shoulder. 'Plenty of what you want? More pudding? Fruit cup?'

'Thanks: we're fine,' said Nicholas.

Roland went through the rest of the evening in a daze, which insulated him from the round of games and dances that followed. By about eleven o'clock everyone was tired of dancing, and nobody could think of any fresh games. They all sat round the room, and it looked as though the last thirty minutes were going to drag into exhaustion.

'I know,' said Jennifer Brodie. 'Let's have a séance! Like we had last Christmas! Please, Jo-jo!'

'Oh, yes! Let's!' several others said.

'Right you are,' said Mr Brodie. 'But don't go scaring yourselves. It's only a parlour game, remember. There's nothing in it.'

'What's a séance?' said Helen.

'Talking to ghosts – table-rapping, and that sort of thing,' said Nicholas.

'I don't want to do it,' said Roland. 'It sounds too creepy.'

'Come on,' said David. 'It's Christmas. And you heard him say it's only a game.'

'Please may we use Grannie's planchette?' Jennifer asked her mother. 'It's more fun with that, and you had it out for your party last night.'

'If you take care of it, darling,' said Mrs Brodie.

'Yes, Mummy.'

There was a conversation between Mr and Mrs Brodie at the door, but all Roland heard was, '– not as if they're old enough – scribble – nothing frightening –'

'Our Grannie was a Spiritualist,' said Robert Brodie. 'And she had this planchette for getting messages from Grandpa. All he ever said was, "Bury me under the river".'

'And did you?' said Nicholas.

'You try it,' said Robert.

Mrs Brodie came back into the room holding a small, heart-shaped board with a pencil sticking through a hole at the pointed end. The board stood on castors so that it could move in any direction.

'The thing is,' said Jennifer, 'that we all sit round the table, and whoever works the planchette lays their right hand on it very gently, and the board travels across the paper on these wheels. The pencil's touching the paper, and so you get what's called Automatic Writing. Only you mustn't watch what you're doing, because it's not you writing. It's the Other Side.'

'Sounds corny, to me,' said Nicholas.

'No, it isn't,' said Jennifer. 'If you try to write deliberately the board skids about. Now who's going to do it?'

'I think it's time young Roland here did his stuff,' said Mr Brodie. 'He's been very quiet all evening.'

'I'd rather not,' said Roland.

'It's only fun,' said Robert.

Roland was hustled to the table, where the planchette was laid on the back of a roll of wallpaper. 'The writing's big,' said Jennifer, 'so you need plenty of room.

'Put your finger tips on the planchette very lightly: that's it. Now everyone sit still. You mustn't speak. Think of nothing. And if the board moves, Roland, don't look at it. It's best if you keep your eyes closed all the time. I'll do the talking bit. Right. Off we go.'

They all sat round the table. Complete silence was impossible. Some of the girls started giggling almost at once.

'Sh!' said Jennifer every few seconds.

'My arm's going numb,' said Roland. 'Can I have a rest?'

'No,' said Jennifer, 'Sh!'

Two minutes went by, and Jennifer cleared her throat.

'Is anyone there?' she said to the ceiling. 'Is anyone there?'

The planchette jerked as if Roland had cramp in his arm, and the pencil made a formless scribble on the wallpaper.

'Is anyone there?' said Jennifer, and she nodded excitedly and stuck her thumb up.

The planchette scribbled again.

'Who is it?'

The planchette moved along the paper in loops like someone's first attempt at writing.

'Not bad, Roland,' said Nicholas.

'I'm not doing anything.'

'Sh!' said Jennifer. 'Who is it?'

'My arm's gone cold,' said Roland. 'I can't feel anything.'

'If you talk you'll spoil it,' said Jennifer. 'Look!'

'What's happening?' said Roland.

Helen squeaked.

'Har, har,' said Nicholas.

'What do you want?' said Jennifer.

The pencil moved.

'What is that?' said Jennifer, speaking precisely.

'An amœba,' said David.

'I do not understand,' said Jennifer.

The pencil scribbled again.

And then,

'I still cannot understand,' said Jennifer. 'Please tell me more.'
The pencil swept across the paper.

And then it wrote,

findhorn

'Findhorn!' cried Helen.

'What?' said Roland. 'What?' The planchette immediately slid away.

'Did it write that? Findhorn? Malebron? This unicorn?'

'Oh, you shouldn't have stopped!' said Jennifer. 'It was coming so well.'

'Enough's enough,' said Mr Brodie.

'He's trying to tell us about Findhorn!' said Roland. 'The Song of Findhorn, remember! Findhorn's a unicorn! He had to keep trying . . .'

'All right, you did it nicely,' said Nicholas. The other guests were staring. 'Your writing's crummy, but you always could draw. You'd be even better with practice.'

'It wasn't me! Try it yourself!'

'OK,' said Nicholas. 'I will.'

He put his fingers on the board as Roland had done.

'Go on, write your name!'

'OK, OK; cool off.'

But no matter how he tried Nicholas could not manage the planchette. It rolled in all directions. One of the boys laughed.

'Here, give it me again,' said Roland. 'He may be wanting to tell us something else. Quick!'

'Er – I think that about wraps things up for tonight, don't you, people?' said Mr Brodie. 'Carriages at eleven-thirty, you know.'

He became brisk and Mrs Brodie removed the

planchette. Everyone started to pick up coats in the hall, and to say thank you. Some were waiting for their parents, and others were being taken home by Mr Brodie. He switched on the outside light, and opened the door to go and bring his car round to the front of the house. A white mist coiled through the doorway into the hall.

'Oh dear, what a bore,' said Mrs Brodie. 'It won't be much fun driving in this. Those who aren't going with John had better take your coats off: your parents may be some time. Put the gramophone on, Jen, and we'll have another dance.'

'I think we'd be quicker walking, don't you?' said Nicholas. 'It's not far.'

'Yes,' said David. 'Really, we mustn't stay, thanks all the same.'

'Can we ring up home to stop Dad from turning out, please?' said Nicholas.

'Certainly,' said Mrs Brodie. 'If you're sure that's what you want to do.'

Nicholas rushed to the telephone. 'Hello, Dad,' he said. 'It's Nick. Look, don't bother to fetch us: we'll walk. No, honest, we'll be home by the time you could get here in this. We'll cut through the new estate and up Boundary Lane – you know, that cinder path by the allotments. Yes, of course I know the way. Yes, we'll borrow a torch. Right. See you in about half an hour.'

They borrowed a torch, but found that there was no need to use it. The mist was a ground mist, and they could see clearly the tops of trees and houses, and the bright moon.

'Anything rather than another dance,' said Nicholas as they went down the drive from the house. 'Well done, Roland. You broke it up nicely. Old Jo-jo thought you were going to throw a fit.'

Roland did not answer.

'How did you pick up the knack of that board so quickly?' said Nicholas.

'Shut up,' said Roland.

'You what?'

'I said shut up.'

'Oh, all right.'

They walked in silence. The concrete road of the new estate was easy to follow, except where it branched, or produced a roundabout. Near the Brodies' house the estate was almost finished. The upstairs windows were dabbed with whitewash. And then farther in, the windows were raw holes, and the moon shone through the roofs. After that there was nothing but the mist, and they followed the kerbstone across what was still a field.

'It – it was a lovely unicorn you drew,' said Helen at last. 'Just like the one on my jug.'

'I didn't draw it,' said Roland.

'Oh, lay off,' said Nicholas.

'Malebron drew it,' said Roland. 'He was trying to tell us something, and you stopped him.'

'Now listen,' said Nicholas. 'It's about time you grew up. Shall I tell you what all that was about? You've got this Malebron thing on the brain. OK, so you didn't fake it on purpose: you wrote it unconsciously, and you drew the unicorn because Helen found the jug when you were digging that hole in the garden. That's how people's minds work. If you'd read the books about it you'd see for yourself you're up the creek.'

'Oh, shut up,' said Roland.

The road ended near a stile that led into the cinder path by the allotments. The path had chestnut palings on one side and a hedge on the other. It ran through a no-man's-land between two built-up areas and came

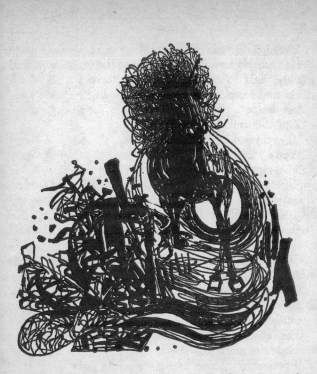

out on the road where the Watsons lived. At one point it crossed a stream over a bridge of railway sleepers.

The path was so narrow that the children had to walk in twos. The night was absolutely still.

'Careful at the bridge,' said David. 'There aren't any hand-rails. We're nearly –'

The sound of air being torn like cloth burst on them, a dreadful sound that cracked with the force of lightning, as if the sky had split, and out of it came the noise of galloping hoofs. There was no warning, no approach: the hoofs were there, in the mist, close to the children, just ahead of them, on top of them, furious.

'Look out!'

They fell sideways against paling and hedge as a white horse charged between them out of the moonlight, pulling the mist to shreds. All about them was hoof and mane and foam, and they heard the horse gallop away along the path and leap the stile into the field.

The children clung to each other.

'Is everyone OK?' said Nicholas.

'Yes.'

'I've ripped my coat.'

'That was a near do,' said David. 'I didn't hear it till it clattered on the bridge, did you?'

'It's probably bolted from the riding school,' said Nicholas.

'It didn't have a saddle on,' said David.

'It's broken out of its stable,' said Helen. 'They wouldn't have left it outside in the winter.'

'Yes,' said Nicholas. 'Did you see the mess it was in? It must have fouled some barbed wire.'

'But wasn't it a beauty?' said David. 'That mane!'

The children crossed the bridge and walked on towards the road.

'I was scared,' said Helen. 'But the poor thing must have been more frightened than I was.'

'It couldn't have stopped,' said Nicholas. 'If we hadn't got out of the way it'd have trampled us to bits. Don't say anything to Mum or Dad: they'd have a heart attack.'

'Gosh, that put the wind up me,' said David.

'Its tail hit me in the face,' said Helen.

'Funny how the moonlight made it look so big, too,' said Nicholas. 'That, and being on a narrow path.'

'I hope it's not in any pain,' said Helen. 'It may do more damage if it's still frightened.'

'It could have killed us,' said David.

'Yes, but not a word,' said Nicholas. They were on the

road now. 'Tidy yourself a bit, Roland. We don't want to look as though we've been beaten up.'

But Roland hung back in the middle of the road.

'Come along, Roland, keep together.'

'Why are you talking like this?' shouted Roland. 'You all saw it! Why are you pretending? You saw the horn on its head!'

16. The Fix

'Come for a walk,' said David.

It was the first time any of the children had spoken to Roland all day. Nicholas had gone off on his bicycle. Helen was careful to stay near her mother about the house, and David had been involved with his wireless textbooks.

'If you like,' said Roland.

They went down the road into Boundary Lane. They crossed the bridge, and then David went back over; stopped; and crossed again.

'OK, Roland,' he said. 'You win.'

'Oh?' said Roland. 'Do I?'

'I know how you feel,' said David, 'but there's no point in sulking. Things are too serious now.'

'What do you mean, "now"?'

'All right, they always have been.'

'Then what's made you change your mind today instead of last night?' said Roland.

'Well, for one thing,' said David, 'the cinders are all cut up by hoof marks on this side of the bridge, but not on the other. Even Nick would have to call that evidence. The unicorn broke through right here.'

'So it was a unicorn?' said Roland.

'Of course it was,' said David. 'And we'll have to do something about it. I'm dead scared.'

'I thought you agreed with Nick.'

'I'd like to,' said David. 'But there was something that didn't fit: it's been bothering me for weeks. It's that static electricity. You see, even if you believe the

Treasures are real and are generators, the static shouldn't be there. And it comes and goes.'

'How do you know?' said Roland.

'Oh, I've been experimenting ever since Dad was on about his roses. It's there most days, early morning or dusk.'

'You didn't tell me!'

'I didn't want to,' said David. 'Anyway, I think I know what's causing it. They're looking for the Treasures in Elidor, and they've found them.'

'Found them!'

'Yes: it's quite simple. It's like getting a radio fix on a transmitter. You have two receivers some distance apart, and they pick up the direction the signal's coming from. Then you draw the two lines on a map, and where they cross is the transmitter.'

'So what?'

'Well, if the Treasures are generating energy that's going through to Elidor, you should be able to get a fix

on them in Elidor. Can't you see what happens next?
They lay this fix, and when they go to the place where the
lines cross there's nothing there! They can point to a
spot in the air, or on the ground, or anywhere, and say,
"That's where the Treasures are", but they can't touch
them!'

'You mean, they can find the place in Elidor which
coincides with our garden, but they can't get through?'
said Roland.

'Exactly. So what do they do? They keep trying to
find the Treasures, and they keep pouring energy into
the same spot, like cracking a safe, but it's not going
anywhere. There's this terrific charge keeps building up
– and some of it leaks through to here as static electricity!'

'If you say so,' said Roland. 'But would they have the
equipment to do it with? It didn't feel as if it's that kind
of place, really.'

'I don't know,' said David. 'But they're managing
somehow.'

'Could they do it with their minds?' said Roland.
'That's how most things seemed to work there.'

'A sort of telepathy?' said David. 'Yes, why not? All
you'd need would be two people to lay the fix, and –'

'Two people?' cried Roland. 'Have you ever seen anything by the roses?'

'No,' said David. 'There's been this static.'

'Listen,' said Roland. 'We've got to prove it to the
others once and for all: now, while they're still jittery
about last night. If I show you you're right, will you
explain to Nick and Helen how it works?'

'Yes: sure. It's only an idea, though. The details may
be wrong.'

'Come on.'

They ran back home.

'What are you going to do?' said David.

'Never mind,' said Roland. 'I'll show you. If nobody knows beforehand then Nick won't be able to talk so much about hallucinations.'

Nicholas was oiling his bicycle when they reached the cottage. David went inside for Helen. She came out looking apprehensive. The afternoon light was fading.

'Now then,' said Roland. 'Last night.'

'I don't want to talk about it,' said Nicholas.

'Why not?'

'I don't, that's all.'

'Why is it so important for you to think Elidor isn't real?' said Roland.

'I'll give you a thick ear in a minute,' said Nicholas.

'What about you, Helen? Do you think we all imagined Elidor?'

'Oh, please, Roland. Let's not row about it: please.'

'Yes, it's stupid to argue,' said Nicholas. 'We can think what we like, but we're here now, and the Treasures, even if they are Treasures, are under the rose bed, and Elidor's finished. It's all over.'

'That's where you're wrong, Nick,' said David. 'You may have finished with Elidor, but Elidor's not finished with us.'

'Whose side are you on?' said Nicholas.

'There aren't any sides,' said David. 'Not after last night.'

'I can explain that,' said Nicholas.

'And can you explain this?' Roland had gone to the rose bed and was holding his hand near one of the bushes. They all heard the crack, and saw the spark jump.

'This once, Nick,' said David. 'Listen to Roland this once. If you're not convinced, I promise we'll not talk about it again.'

'Oh,' said Nicholas, 'anything for a quiet life. What's he going to do?'

'I don't know.'

Again Roland had felt the charge as abruptly as if it had been switched on, and he arranged everybody in a tight group on the lawn facing the spot where the shadows had appeared.

'Can you feel the static electricity?' he said.

'I don't like it,' said Helen. 'It's giving me goose-flesh.'

'Watch the rose bed. And keep watching,' said Roland.

'Are you sure you know what you're doing?' said David.

'My neck's aching,' said Helen.

'Don't move. Keep watching,' said Roland. Oh, where are they? They must come. Nick's got to see them –

'So it's static electricity,' said Nicholas. 'It's happened before.'

'You're telling me!' said David. 'But it's getting stronger. I'm all pins and needles. We must be in some kind of energy field.'

Just once more, and never again. It was as strong as this last time. They must come. They must, they must – That's it! 'There! Look!'

The two shadows stood on the rose bed.

'You fool!' groaned David. 'You've done it now. It's the fix!'

'But that's what I've always seen,' said Roland. 'What about it, Nick? Go on, have a good look. You can walk round them.'

Nicholas made a strangled noise in his throat.

'Is this one of your hallucinations, eh?' said Roland, and tried to turn his head to see how Nicholas was re-acting. But his neck muscles were locked. The shadows darkened.

'I can't move!' said Helen. 'I can't move! Oh, my neck!'

'It's all right,' said Roland. 'They go away if you leave them.'

'You cretin!' said David. 'They're using us! Shut your eyes! Don't look!'

'I can still see them! In my head!' cried Helen.

The air whined. The shadows were pools fringed with light, no longer in the garden, no longer anywhere: free of space, they had no depth and no end.

'I didn't mean it,' said Roland. 'I only wanted to show you – so you'd know.'

He could hardly speak for the numbness that welled through him. His strength was being sucked out.

'Can't you stop them?' whimpered Helen. 'Oh, look! – Look!'

A white spot had appeared in the middle of each shadow, quivering like a focused beam of light. The spots grew, lessened their intensity, changed, congealed, and became the expanding forms of two men, rigid as dolls, hurtling towards the children. They matched the outlines of the shadows, and were rising like bubbles to their surface. As they came nearer their speed increased: they rushed upon the children, and filled the shadows, and eclipsed them – and at that instant they lost their woodenness and stepped, two men of Elidor, into the garden.

They were dressed in tunics and cloaks and carried spears. Shields hung on their backs. They were bewildered, and stood as if they had woken in the middle of a dream. Then they both looked at the soil between them where the Treasures were buried.

There was no static electricity in the air, and the hold on the children disappeared.

The men lifted their eyes, stared round at the garden,

and then ran across the lawn and swung themselves over the fence into the orchard next door. Helen, David, and Roland did not move, but Nicholas broke forward after the men. He snatched up stones and threw them wildly into the trees. He was sobbing.

17. Spear-edge and Shield-rim

'You're not safe loose,' said David. 'You need locking up.'

'I didn't know what it was,' said Roland. 'And you wouldn't listen to me. I had to show you. It's Nick's fault as much as mine.'

'You're so mad keen to be proved right, you'd do anything, wouldn't you?' said David.

'Save your breath,' said Nicholas. 'We've got to decide what to do.'

'There's nothing we can do,' said David. 'This raving nit has seen to that. We might as well hand over the Treasures before one of us gets a spear in his back.'

'Look: all I've ever wanted is to be left alone,' said Nicholas. 'I thought if we dropped this Elidor business we'd be all right. So fair enough, I'm to blame as much as Roland. My way hasn't worked. Have you got a better one?'

Nobody said anything.

'Then how about this?' said Nicholas. 'We can't fool ourselves any longer, so let's do the opposite. Let's go out and bash them first, before they bash us.'

'But they've got spears,' said Roland.

'I didn't mean it that way,' said Nicholas. 'It's the Treasures they're after: right? They're not really interested in us.'

'You can't give them the Treasures!' said Roland. 'You can't let Elidor die like that! You can't! It's the most important thing there is!'

'If I thought it'd help,' said Nicholas, 'I'd hand the

Treasures over. But those two would still be here, and so would the Treasures. When they came out of their shadows they'd no more idea of where they were than we had when we landed in Elidor. If they can't find a way back with the Treasures there'll be more coming after them. But if the Treasures are in Elidor, we'll be left in peace.'

'Fine,' said David. 'But how do you get the Treasures into Elidor?'

'Search me,' said Nicholas.

'Malebron won't have a hope,' said Roland.

'That's his problem,' said Nicholas. 'We didn't volunteer for this.'

'Nick's right,' said David. 'We can't hide them, and we can't fight for them.'

'What about the unicorn?' said Helen.

'That's what I mean,' said Nicholas. 'When you start messing around with these things, you don't know where it'll end. We'll have half of Elidor in our back garden if we're not quick.'

'But that was Findhorn,' said Roland. 'He was being hunted. You saw those gashes all down his side. He had to break into our world to escape. They want to kill him before Malebron can find him. Malebron was trying to tell us. There's something he wants us to do.'

'Then he can want,' said Nicholas.

It was clear the following morning that there was not much time. During the night, slates had been taken from the coalhouse roof, and their fragments littered the rose bed. They had been used as spades, but the frozen ground had broken them.

Mrs Watson was too busy to notice anything all day. She had an appointment at the hairdresser's in the afternoon, and then she was going into Manchester to meet Mr Watson. They were having dinner with some friends before the New Year dance, which was being held at a large hotel in the middle of the city.

'What'll be the next move?' said David.

'They'll come back tonight with something to dig up the Treasures,' said Nicholas. 'It'll be easy enough. There are plenty of garden sheds round here. I think we're pretty safe in daylight, though. They'll be lying up till it's dark.'

'So we lift the Treasures first, is that it?' said David.

'Yes: we'll have about an hour after Mum leaves before it starts to freeze.'

'What's Dad going to say when he sees the mess?'

'It needn't be a mess,' said Nicholas. 'We can stick the bushes in again, and we'll throw the earth on to a couple of ground sheets.'

Helen drew a sketch plan of the rose bed and labelled the bushes so that they could be replanted. Tools and ground sheets were made ready.

'Now are you sure you can look after yourselves?' said Mrs Watson. 'There's cold meat and pickles, and be sensible about going to bed, won't you? Don't sit up all night in front of the television, and fetch the coal in before dark, and put the fire guard up. The hotel's phone number is on the pad.'

'Stop flapping, Mum,' said David. 'We'll be all right.'

'You'll miss the train,' said Nicholas.

'Oh, heavens! Is that the time? Oh, I sometimes wonder if it's worth the fuss. I wouldn't go if your father wasn't so set on it.'

'Good-bye, Mum,' said Helen. 'Have a lovely time.'

The children watched their mother until she was out of sight round the corner of the road.

'Phew,' said Nicholas.

They dug in relays without a pause.

The knots in the flex tying the lid to the dustbin had swollen, and they had to wait while David rummaged upstairs for his wire cutters. The polythene bags were milky with condensation when the children pulled them out of the bin, but the Treasures seemed to be no different for their year underground.

The children dropped the dustbin back, and trod the soil down as it was shovelled into the hole. The rose bushes were more or less straight.

'I think we ought to put the Treasures under our beds for tonight,' said David after tea, 'and try and get rid of them tomorrow.'

'Yes, but how?' said Nicholas.

'That's it,' said David. 'We're lumbered. Have you any brilliant schemes, Roland?'

Roland shook his head.

David switched on the television set. 'And it must be tomorrow,' he said. 'Remember this?' As the set warmed up, the screeching and whistling began, and the picture, when it came, was a herringbone of black and white. 'It won't be long before Dad's razor starts, either. There'll be fun tonight.'

'They look so harmless, don't they?' said Helen. 'This cup: it's ugly: nothing like that bowl with pearls all round it, and full of light.'

'But can't you feel that they're still the Treasures?' said Roland. 'They're still the same.'

'Yes, I suppose you're right,' said David. 'The real sword and these two bits of wood have the same kind of "swordness" about them. That's not changed.'

'Let's try it,' said Helen. 'I'll go and bring an ordinary cup from the kitchen, and we'll see if there's any difference.'

'For crying out loud!' said Nicholas. 'Are you all off your rockers? – There! And I bet it's Mum's best china!'

They had heard a cup smash on the floor in the kitchen. Helen came running through the middle room and slammed the door behind her.

'I was – I was taking a cup,' she said, 'off the – the shelf. And someone – lifted the latch on the back door. It went up – and down. I'd never have heard it: it was so quiet.'

'Is the door bolted?' said Nicholas.

'Yes.'

'But you'd hear anyone coming round the side of the house.'

'I didn't. Nothing. Somebody tried the latch. I couldn't hear it.'

'They know we've got 'em,' said David. 'Obviously. They'd know straight away.'

'Wait a minute,' said Nicholas. 'Keep calm.'

'Dial 999,' said David.

But before he could say any more there was the sound of falling glass in the middle room.

'Out of the way!' shouted Nicholas.

He pushed Helen aside and threw open the door. A window pane had been broken, and a thin arm was feeling for the latch inside. The telephone was on the window-sill.

Nicholas grabbed the poker from the hearth and crashed it down on the arm. There was a howl, and the arm jerked out of sight.

'Everybody here, quick!' said Nicholas. 'Shove the dresser across! And the other window! Stack the chairs on the table in front of it!'

'What about the kitchen?' said David.

'Leave that. Only the fanlight opens. Now bring your

coats and the rucksack into the other room. Hurry! I'll put the light off in here.'

'Nick: what'll we do?' said Helen, when they were together in the sittingroom.

'Quiet a minute,' said Nicholas.

He went to the front door and listened at the curtain.

'There's one of them in the porch. We can't keep them out. The dresser and the chairs will hold them up a bit, but that's all. We've got to move. We'll be safe in a crowd, or where there's plenty of light. They won't risk being caught.'

'Where'll we go?'

'Anywhere. It doesn't matter.'

Nicholas packed the stone in the rucksack. 'Here, give me your cup,' he said to Helen. 'There's room for it.'

'No,' said Helen. 'I'll carry it. I'd rather.'

'Please yourself. Now listen. Have we any money?'

'I've some from Christmas,' said Roland.

'So have I,' said Helen.

'How do we get out, first?' said David.

'We'll crunch him behind the door,' said Nicholas. 'Like Dad, only better. We wait till we hear the other one climb through, and when he's sorting himself out from the furniture we'll flatten this one against the porch and run for it. Mind you don't trip over the curtain.'

'Here he comes,' said David.

The dresser pitched forward on to the floor.

'Ready?'

'Mum's Willow Pattern,' said Helen.

There was the sound of scuffling, and more glass tinkled, and then someone fell heavily over the dresser.

'Now!'

Nicholas slipped the catch. They thrust their shoulders against the door and lashed it open. They felt the resil-

ience of a body trapped between the door and the wall.
A man cried out. And the children were running down
the middle of the road, their legs hammering the
smooth surface till their thighs burned.

Roland glanced over his shoulder and saw a figure
lope from the porch and cross the lamplight to the darkness of the hedge along the footpath.

'They're coming!'

'Make a row! Fetch people out!'

'Help!'

'Help!'

Helen screamed.

'Help! Help!'

Lights were switched off all down the road.

'Help! Help!'

Visitors were leaving one house, but they stepped back,
and shut the door. On the other side of the dimpled
glass a broken pattern of a man reached up to slide the
bolt.

'Please! Help!'

Christmas trees in front windows disappeared as the
curtains swirled across.

'You lousy rotten devils!' yelled David.

'Keep moving!'

The children ran from pool to pool of the street lamps
and sometimes they glimpsed a shadow, and sometimes
there was a tall silhouette: and there was always too
much darkness. When they turned the corner the white
fluorescence of the railway station at the end of the road
was like a sanctuary. They drove themselves towards its
glass and concrete, as if the danger behind, the danger
of spear-edge and shield-rim, would be powerless in the
neon glare.

They jostled through the barrier on to the platform. An
electric train was idling its motor: the porter was waving

to the guard, and when he saw the children he opened a
door.

'Come on, come on, if you want it.'

They were carried forward by the impetus of their
running, and almost all the porter had to do was to
deflect them by the arm into the compartment, one after
the other, like dominoes falling.

'Right away!'

The train glided out of the station, and quickly
gathered speed.

18. *Paddy*

' "Right away",' said David. ' "Right away"! As easy as that!'

'Too easy,' said Roland.

'How do you mean?'

Roland pulled a face. 'Too easy: I dunno.'

'I thought we'd had it then,' said Helen. 'I could feel those spears. Any second, I thought.'

'We were lucky,' said Nicholas.

'Yes, we were,' said Roland, 'weren't we?'

'How far shall we go?' said David.

'All the way,' said Nicholas. 'Into Manchester. It's safest.'

'We'd better tell Mum and Dad,' said Helen.

'I'd like to see you try,' said Nicholas. 'We'll say there was someone breaking in, so we cleared out. There'll be enough of a shambles to prove we weren't kidding.'

'And then what?' said David. 'There's the rest of the night left for the Treasures to be pinched. What time does the dance end?'

'One o'clock.'

'Right. We shan't do anything now. We'll meet Mum and Dad out of the dance, and then it'll be three o'clock at least before the fuss is over. With luck, we'll not go to bed at all.'

They paid their fare at the terminus, and walked down the long slope from the station into the city. The streets were brilliant with lights and decorations. People hurried along in groups, making a lot of noise, and very cheerful.

'We want the cheapest place to keep warm in while

we're waiting,' said Nicholas. 'Let's try a coffee bar.'

The children sat at wrought-iron tables in a room that was all bamboo and rubber plant. Non-stop South American music came from a loudspeaker and was killed by the gush of the coffee machine. The children sat there for an hour, ordering more coffee when the waitress glared hard enough.

'It's not going to be cheap, at this rate,' said Nicholas.

'I'm still jumpy,' said Helen. 'I feel as though everybody's watching us, though I know they're not.'

'Me too,' said David. 'And we ought to move. We're not all that safe. It's about a three-hour walk into Manchester from our house: give them another hour to allow for dodging people: so they'll be arriving about two hours from now. They'll home on to the Treasures wherever we are. The only thing to do is to stay on the move, then they won't be able to lay a fix so easily.'

'I know!' said Roland. 'Let's ride on buses. If we keep changing, they'll never track us down.'

'That's it,' said David.

They drank their coffee and went out into the street.

'Which one?' said Helen. 'There are dozens.'

'Any bus'll do,' said Roland. 'The first that stops. There! That Number 76!'

They ran along the pavement to the bus stop.

'Inside,' said the conductor, a West Indian. 'Plenty of room inside.'

The children took the front two seats behind the driver. Nicholas put the rucksack on his lap.

'Where do you go?' said David.

'Brookdale Park,' said the conductor.

'One and three halves all the way, please,' said Nicholas.

The bus crawled round the city centre. The traffic was dense, and people were using the streets as footpaths, but in a short while the Christmas glitter dropped behind. The bus was passing through an area of garages, public houses, and government-surplus stores.

'It's a bit grim up this end, isn't it?' said David.

'Don't you know where we are?' said Roland. 'We've just turned off Oldham Road. We're near Thursday Street.'

The bus stopped. 'Hurry along, please,' said the conductor. 'Both sides.'

'Shoor, a little bit of Heaven – fell-l-l – from out the sky one day – !'

The voice sang, blurred and loud, on the platform. The children looked round, and saw the conductor help a big Irishman up the step. He caught at the overhead rail, missed, and slumped heavily on to the back seat. He wore an army greatcoat, and he was very drunk.

'Man, you started your New Year early,' said the conductor.

'Good luck,' said the Irishman.

'Where you for?'

'Home.'

'I don't know where that is. You tell me.'

'Ballymartin, County Down.' He was staring straight ahead of him. 'There's a rocky old road I would follow,' he sang, 'to a place that is Heaven to me. Though it's never so grand, still it's my fairyland –'

'We don't go there, man. Brookdale Park any good?'

The Irishman held a ten shilling note between his fingers. The conductor took the note, and put a ticket and the change in the Irishman's coat pocket.

The other passengers were trying to ignore him. They became interested in their newspapers, or the advertisements in the bus, or the view from the window.

The Irishman hung over the back of the next seat. 'Eh, missus,' he said to the woman sitting there. 'Missus.'

She froze. 'Good luck,' said the Irishman, and appeared to go to sleep.

The woman moved, and went upstairs. At once the Irishman lurched round and sat on the edge of the empty seat. His shoulder filled the gangway. He leaned forward to tap the arm of the man in front.

'Eh, guv'nor.'

David gasped. 'Don't look!' he whispered to the others. 'Don't let him see your faces! It's him! Paddy, from the demolition gang!'

The children shrank in their seats and used the window behind the driver as a mirror.

'And we've still got the Treasures!' said Helen. 'He'll murder us!'

'Would he remember?' said David. 'It's more than a year ago, and he's properly sloshed.'

'If someone had swiped me with an iron railing, I'd not forget 'em,' said Nicholas. 'Stick your head down, Roland.'

Paddy tried again. 'Eh, guv'nor. Have yez a piece of paper I could be writin' on?' The man twitched his arm away. 'Oh, it may be for yeeeears –' sang Paddy, 'and it may be for ever – !' The man stood up, and pushed past him.

'Ruddy Micks!' he said.

'Good luck,' said Paddy, and moved forward another seat.

'Here, you wanting paper?' said the conductor. 'I got some you can have.' He tore a couple of sheets out of a notebook and gave them to Paddy.

'That's dacent,' said Paddy. He felt in his pockets and fished out a stump of pencil, and became absorbed in trying to write on his knee in the swaying bus.

'Brookdale Park!' shouted the conductor. The bus stopped, and the engine was switched off. The con-

ductor went round to talk to the driver. The children and Paddy were the only people left.

'Shall we run for it?' said David.

'Not a hope,' said Nicholas. 'We couldn't get past him.'

'Eh?' said Paddy. 'Are yez there, then?' He strained to focus on the children, hauled himself upright, and crashed down again on the seat opposite Nicholas.

'Eh, a-vic,' he said. 'Would yez be helpin' me with this letter?'

'Er – yes: sure,' said Nicholas.

'I'm not the illiterate, yez'll understand. I can put a letter together with the best of them. Oh, yes. But it's a terrible night I've had. A terrible night.'

There was no recognition.

'Yes, of course. What do you want me to do?' Nicholas relaxed his grip on the rucksack.

'I'm resignin',' said Paddy. 'Oh, they don't see me again. It's me letter of resignation. If I tell yez what to say, will yez be puttin' it down? Ah – eh – "To the foreman. Dear Sir. – Dear Sir". Eh – have yez written that?'

'Yes,' said Nicholas.

'Ah, well then. "Dear Sir." Oh, it's a terrible night.'

'Is that in the letter?' said Nicholas.

'Eh? Oh, no. No. "Dear Sir, Herewith me resignation" – That's good: that's good – "me resignation I won't be comin' no more it's no place for a good Catholic yours truly Mr Patrick Mehigan".'

'Do you want to sign it?' said Nicholas.

'No. Eh, no. No. Leave it, a-vic.'

Paddy took the letter, folded it, and stared at it in silence. Nicholas was about to give a signal for them to creep away, when Paddy spoke.

'Am I drunk?'

'I beg your pardon,' said Nicholas.

'I said, am I drunk?'

'Er – perhaps: a little.'

'And no wonder,' said Paddy. 'But is horses with horns any sight for a workin' man?'

'What?' cried Roland. 'Where? Where did you see it?'

'Hello there,' said Paddy. 'It's a terrible night.'

Roland bobbed on the seat. 'When? Was it today? Here?'

'Lay off him,' said David. 'He can't follow you. Hey, Paddy: tell us about it. We're listening.'

'Arragh: yez'll not believe me.'

'We shall. I promise. Please, Paddy.'

'Well then,' said Paddy, 'yez'll understand it's not a livin' wage on this job if yez can't make a bit extra on the side, like. So I'm goin' back after dark to pick up the odd scrap or two of lead I'd seen lyin' about the place. So there's this yard where I've put a few pieces by under an old bath, see? So I goes in – and there's this horse, all white, and this horn on its head yez could hardly stand up for the sight of. Well, as soon as it has wind of me it's away out of it, and divil a care whether I shifts or no, right past me, and there's me on me back. There now. Yez'll not believe that.'

'Don't worry,' said Nicholas. 'We believe you.'

'Yez'll not believe it,' said Paddy. 'I didn't meself.' He reached inside his coat and pulled out a wallet. 'But when I'm in the pub afterwards, recoverin' like, I find these caught in me buttons.' He opened the wallet, and lying between two ragged envelopes were a few wisps of hair.

The children had never seen anything like them. They were neither white nor silver. They were strands of pure light.

Roland caught his breath. 'Let me hold them,' he said.

'Oh, no,' said Paddy, drawing back. 'I'll not let no one touch them. There's no luck in it. I has a drink to see if they'll go away, but they won't. I takes a peep after every drink, but they're still there. Oh, it's a terrible night.'

'Hi, you waiting for something?' said the conductor. 'It's the end of the road, man.'

'The same again, please,' said Roland.

'It's a free country,' said the conductor. 'But where's he going?'

'Home to Ballymartin,' said Paddy. 'I'll not be stayin' here.'

'We want the stop where he got on,' said Roland, holding out the money.

'Wait a minute –' said David.

'OK,' said the conductor. He took Paddy's fare out of his coat pocket and put another ticket in.

'Good luck,' said Paddy, and began to read his letter. It was upside down, but he admired it.

The bus left them at the corner of a gaslit street. Paddy seemed to be feeling better for the ride.

'Will you show us where you saw this horse?' said Roland.

'I will not,' said Paddy.

'Hold on, Roland,' said David.

'Please,' said Roland.

'I'll show yez the way, but I'll not go.'

'Me neither,' said Helen.

They walked to the next corner, and Paddy stopped by instinct outside the frosted glass door of a public house.

'If yez goes on down the next street,' he said, 'yez'll be near enough.' His attention was wandering, drawn to the sound of a piano and laughter from the other side of the door. 'Eh – I think I'll be havin' a drop to keep out the cold,' he said. 'It's been a terrible night.'

He pushed open the door. Noise swamped the pavement and he disappeared among the faces, smoke, heat, and din of the public house. The door swung shut.

The children stayed on the corner. Ahead of them the street was a tunnel: no lamps were lit: the houses were empty.

19. The Wasteland

' "Coincidence"!' said Roland. 'That's all you can say. "Coincidence." You make me sick!'

'Well, if you think we're trapesing round in that hole,' said David, 'you can think again.'

'But if we find him everything will be all right,' said Roland.

'I'm too scared,' said Helen.

'You landed us in enough trouble yesterday with your hen-brained ideas,' said David. 'We're not going. And that's flat.'

'Oh yes we are!' said Roland – and sprinted for the blacked-out street.

'Roland! You great steaming chudd! Come back!'

The voices died behind him.

They'll have to come now! They daren't leave me!

He ran along the wider streets until his eyes were used to the dark. The moon had risen, and the glow of the city lightened the sky. He twisted down alleyways, running blindly, through cross-roads, over bombed sites, and along the streets again.

I'll find 'em when they're right in. It'll be easy. They'll be calling after me.

The iron railing was heavy. He carried it hanging at arm's length, and it was beginning to pull his shoulder down. Roland stopped, and listened. There was only the noise of the city, a low, constant rumble that was like silence.

He was in the demolition area. Roof skeletons made broken patterns against the sky.

Now that he was tired Roland felt less sure of himself.
But at the time it had seemed the only thing to do. He
had looked at the three stubborn faces, and had known
that he could not argue with them any more. It was not
a matter of disbelief. They believed him: but they were
frightened. And Roland was frightened, too.

The streets were so quiet. His footsteps echoed on the
cobbles. The ruins hemmed him in. Doors and windows
stared at him: abandoned furniture crouched among
the rubble. A tin can rattled down a pile of bricks in the
shadow of a building.

'Here!' Roland called. 'I'm here!'

No answer.

Roland went on. The difficulty was that he could

never see far in any direction because of the streets. The whole place was a maze of right-angles. The other children might be near, but he would miss them, and he was not going to shout again.

Roland searched for a place that would be safe to climb, and found a staircase on the exposed inner wall of a house. The top step was the highest part of the house: everything above it, including the bedroom floor, had been knocked down.

Roland tested his weight, but the wood was firm, so he went up.

He could see little more of the streets from the top than from the ground. Behind him was a double row of back yards. The entry between them showed as a cleft.

They're bound to come sooner or later, thought Roland. The best thing is to stay put.

He sat on the top of the stairs in the moonlight. It was freezing hard. Roofs and cobbles sparkled. Roland felt better. The menace left the streets, and instead he was aware of the quietness as something poised, as if he could always sit here under the moon.

But the cold began to ache into him. He wondered if the others had decided to stay in one place and to wait until he came.

This thought bothered him, and he was still trying to make up his mind when the unicorn appeared at the end of the street.

He was moving at a fast trot, and he wheeled about at the cross-road, unsure of the way. Then he came on towards Roland.

Roland sat there above the street and watched the unicorn pass below him, and he dared not even breathe.

The unicorn turned aside to pause at entries and gaps in the walls. He would stand at the threshold of a house, one hoof raised, but always he swung away, and on down the street.

His mane flowed like a river in the moon: the point of the horn drew fire from the stars. Roland shivered with the effort of looking. He wanted to fix every detail in his mind for ever, so that no matter what else happened there would always be this.

The unicorn turned into the next street, and Roland lost him until he heard the clatter of rubble in the entry, and there was the high neck moving between the walls.

He hurried down the stairs as quietly as he could, and groped his way through the house to the yard. He climbed over the entry wall as the unicorn reached the far end. Roland went after him.

The entry finished in a square of earth and cinders completely enclosed by walls. The unicorn had heard Roland and was waiting, alert, in the middle of the square. They both stood motionless, watching each other.

'Findhorn,' said Roland. 'Findhorn.'

The unicorn tossed his head. Roland walked forward very slowly.

'Findhorn. Sing – Findhorn.'

He was within twenty feet of the unicorn. The nostrils flared.

'Sing, Findhorn.'

The unicorn stamped his hoof and his ears dropped flat to his skull. Roland halted.

'You must sing! You've got to!'

He took a step forward, and the horn plunged towards him. Roland dodged aside, and the unicorn went by at a canter, heading for the entry.

'No!' shouted Roland, and ran after the unicorn. 'Wait! You mustn't go!' He caught up with him and tried to turn him. 'Hey! Hey! Hey!' He waved his arm. The unicorn stopped. 'Woa back!' He recognised the lowering of the neck, and moved in time. Still the unicorn did not follow up the thrust, but carried on towards the entry.

'Wait!' Roland blocked the way. 'Findhorn! Sing!' And he flourished the iron railing, the spear, in the unicorn's face.

The silver body grew black against the sky as the unicorn reared and brought his hoofs thrashing down. Roland flung himself sideways, and the hoofs showered him with frozen grit. He scrambled on all fours. 'No, Findhorn!' But the unicorn was on him, cruel and merciless. Round and round, spraying cinders: only Roland's agility saved him: hoofs and horn and teeth: round and round.

There could be no end to it, no escape. Roland's nerve failed. He ran for the wall.

'Jump!'

He heard the voice, and through sweat he saw a hunchbacked shape kneeling on the broad coping stone of the wall. 'Catch hold!' An arm reached, and he leapt, grabbed, and half swung, half clawed himself up the wall.

'You never learn, do you?' said Nicholas. The stone in the rucksack on his shoulders had nearly overbalanced him when he took Roland's weight. They lay together, not daring to move, while the horn flashed below them.

'Where've you come from?' gasped Roland.

'I was in the street on the other side, and I heard you beefing.'

'We've got to make him sing,' said Roland. 'It's the way to save Elidor. That's what we're here for.'

'What?' said Nicholas. 'That? Sing? Don't make me laugh!'

'He must. He's got to. He's frightened: you can't blame him.'

The unicorn was pacing backwards and forwards under the wall.

'He doesn't seem frightened to me,' said Nicholas. 'I'd say he wanted to finish us off.'

'That's because he saw the spear. He thinks he's being hunted again. Look at those scars all along his flank.'

'He doesn't give up, does he?' said Nicholas. 'I'm glad we don't have to go down there.'

'But we do,' said Roland. 'I dropped the spear when I jumped.'

'That's that, then,' said Nicholas. 'We'll have to get by on three Treasures. But why is the unicorn here in the first place?'

'Trying to go back, I think,' said Roland. 'He knows this is one of the gates through. I was watching him in the street.'

'Have you seen David and Helen?'

'No,' said Roland. 'Aren't they with you?'

'We lost each other crossing a bombed site.'

'Oh.'

'Yes, you've made a right mess of things one way or another,' said Nicholas.

'We must find them,' said Roland.

'You don't say! Well, where are they?'

Nicholas swept his arm to include the whole city. The row of houses they were on was at the edge of the demolition area. On the other side from where the unicorn was waiting lay the open wasteland.

Roland looked across the frozen landscape. He started, nearly falling off the wall.

'There!' he said. 'There they are!'

Two figures were running together towards the houses.

'Thank goodness for that,' said Nicholas. 'Ahoy! David! Helen! Here!'

'Hello!' shouted a voice.

'That's David!' said Roland. 'He's in the street!'

'Then who are those two?' said Nicholas.

But by now the figures were near enough for Roland and Nicholas to see the cloaks, and the moon gleamed on the spears in the wasteland.

20. The Song of Findhorn

David's head poked through the back window of a house.

'So you've collared the little twerp,' he said. 'Where was he?'

'Up here, quick,' said Nicholas.

'I'll wring your neck for you one of these days, Roland,' said David. 'Is Helen with you?'

'No. Stop waffling, and get up here quick!' said Nicholas. David stepped over the window-sill into the yard, and climbed the bank of rubbish that was piled against the wall. Roland and Nicholas gave him a hand up on to the coping stone.

'What are you doing here?' said David. 'Oh, crumbs!' He found himself looking straight down at the unicorn.

'That's not the only thing,' said Nicholas. 'Have you seen what's coming?'

The two men were near the edge of the wasteland, heading straight for the children.

'Happy New Year,' said David. 'Let's nip along the wall to the other side of this square.'

'I can't leave the spear,' said Roland.

'You'll have one all to yourself soon enough if we don't shift,' said Nicholas.

They began to move along the wall. Findhorn kept pace with them below.

'Roland wants him to sing,' said Nicholas. 'Then we can all go home.'

'You're stark raving bonkers,' said David.

'But he must sing,' said Roland. 'It was in that book.

"And the Darkness shall not fade unless there is heard the Song of Findhorn." It's prophecy. He has to sing!'

'No, he hasn't,' said David. ' "Unless" doesn't mean he's going to. It doesn't even mean that he can. Sing? You go down there and we'll see who does the singing!'

'Watch out,' said Nicholas. 'They're here.'

The men were on the wall across the corner of the square.

David brandished the lath sword. 'Treasures! Stinking bits of wood!'

'Into this house and through the yard,' said Nicholas.

'What if the door's blocked?' said David. 'Some are.'

'Wait,' said Roland. 'They've seen Findhorn.'

And the unicorn had seen the men. He veered from the wall towards the centre of the square, snorting, tearing the earth, levelling his horn, showing fury.

The men unslung their shields before dropping into the square.

'They're going to kill him to stop him from singing!' cried Roland.

The men separated. They threw their spears from a distance, and then advanced with swords.

'Findhorn! Run! Don't stay! Run!'

But Findhorn showed no sign of flight. He gathered himself to charge.

'They've been trying to kill him all along. That's why he was being hunted. They know he can sing!'

The men came on. Findhorn swung his head, uncertain which to attack. The men crouched. And Findhorn launched himself at them. The man he attacked did not fight, but jumped aside, and the other sprang in and struck at Findhorn, tearing a gash down the shoulder, and when Findhorn whipped round, the first man thrust in to the side. And this way they played the

unicorn so that he could never follow up his charge. The men were round him like dogs. From the wall it looked as if they juggled with lightning.

'You have to admire their guts,' said David. 'I wouldn't go down there for anyone – especially if I was

after the Treasures and there were just three kids to deal
with. Though I suppose they know they can mop us up
any day of the week.'

'Where are you off to, Roland?' said Nicholas.

Roland was walking back along the wall. 'It's all right,'
he said.

'I bet it is. You come here.'

Roland began to run, his arms outstretched for balance. He heard Nicholas start after him but he did not look. He was trying to find the place where he had jumped on to the wall.

The men were working Findhorn into a corner. Roland sat on the edge of the coping stone, twisted on to his stomach, lowered himself, and dropped.

He landed in the dark of the wall close to the fighting. He scrabbled in the dirt for the railing, and found it. Nicholas was above him, but the height was too much for a standing jump, and as Roland lifted the railing one of the men glanced towards the wall. He turned back to the fight, gave one slash with his sword, and came for Roland.

Nicholas slithered down into the yard on the other side of the wall. He heaved at the flat iron bar that bolted the door: it moved, and Roland fell inside. Nicholas rammed the bar back into its socket. A man's warning shout was torn away by rushing hoofs, there was one loud scream outside the door, and the door was split by a horn. It stood out above Roland's head.

The horn jerked back, and the wood groaned, and a weight slumped against the door on the other side.

David was on the coping stone, looking into the square.

'He didn't have a chance,' he said. 'As soon as he took his eyes off it, it got him. Right through his shield, and everything.'

Roland and Nicholas joined David on the wall. While Findhorn had been pulling himself clear the other man had fled for the entry. He could not face the unicorn alone.

Findhorn charged.

'Don't lose him!' said David. 'Try and warn Helen – she can't be far off! And watch out! He whipped a spear!'

'If she tangles with either of them she's a goner,' said Nicholas. 'Just remember that, Roland. Just in case.'

The unicorn had been so far ahead that they rushed out of the entry into the street, thinking they would catch no more than a glimpse at a corner. But they nearly ran into him.

All three scattered for cover.

The unicorn was careering up and down the street, silver and dark with wounds.

'He's gone berserk!' shouted David.

'I think he can still smell the man,' said Nicholas. 'He could be anywhere.'

'It's hardly real!' said David. 'All fire and air!'

Findhorn spun on his hind legs and his nostrils smoked in the frost. And Helen walked round the corner of the street. She stopped in the middle of the cobbles when she saw the unicorn. She was holding the cup in both hands.

'Helen! Look out! Get behind a wall or something!'

Findhorn went down the street like a wind of flame. Helen seemed unable to move.

And then Findhorn checked, and shied, and halted. He raised his head and walked delicately towards Helen, and when he reached her he left all his fierceness, and knelt before her, and lay down. Helen knelt, too, and he put his great head in her lap.

'It's all right,' Roland called softly. 'He won't hurt you.'

'I know,' said Helen.

Roland climbed down, and walked up the street. Nicholas shouted something after him, but he did not hear.

'What is it, Roland?' said Helen. 'Oh, what is it?'

She was looking into Findhorn's eyes.

' "Save maid that is makeless, no man with me mell",' whispered Roland.

Helen began to cry silently.

'I've broken it,' she said.

'Sing, Findhorn,' said Roland. 'Please sing.'

The unicorn stared up at Helen, and for the first time Roland looked into his eyes. What he saw he could not describe: it was almost too strong to bear.

'Findhorn: Findhorn. You must sing. Everything will be all right if you sing. No one will be able to hunt you. You'll be safe. Please. Sing.'

He heard David and Nicholas come and stand behind him. Findhorn did not move. All his strength slept.

'You can save Elidor. I know you can. I know now. Sing, Findhorn.'

A brick crashed into the street. Down one side, only the front of the terrace remained, and the man was coming along the top of the wall, his spear raised. Behind him the city glowed.

David and Nicholas closed round the unicorn, but there was nothing they could do.

'Sing!' cried Roland. 'Before it's too late! You'll be killed!'

Findhorn strove almost as if to speak, but he could not, and he could not.

The man paused: balanced himself to throw.

'Sing: oh, sing.'

Helen cradled his head, and stroked the curls of light.

'Up!' shouted Roland. 'Up! Findhorn! Run! Oh, Findhorn! Findhorn! No!'

The spear hissed down, and sank between the unicorn's ribs to the heart. The white neck arched, and the head lifted to the stars and gave tongue of fire that rang

beyond the streets, the city, the cold hills and the sky. The worlds shook at the song.

A brightness grew on the windows of the terrace, and in the brightness was Elidor, and the four golden castles. Behind Gorias a sun-burst swept the land with colour. Streams danced, and rivers were set free, and all the shining air was new. But a mist was covering Findhorn's eyes.

'Now!' said Nicholas. 'Now's our chance! Give them back now!'

He broke the straps on the rucksack to pull at the stone.

The song went on, a note of beauty and terror.

Roland looked through the windows out over Elidor. He saw the tall figure on the battlements of Gorias, with the golden cloak about him. He saw the life spring in the land from Mondrum to the mountains of the north. He saw the morning. It was not enough.

'Yes! Take them!'

He cried his pain, and snatching the cup from Helen, he threw it and the railing at the windows. Nicholas and David threw their Treasures. They struck together, and the windows blazed outwards, and for an instant the glories of stone, sword, spear, and cauldron hung in their true shapes, almost a trick of the splintering glass, the golden light.

The song faded.

The children were alone with the broken windows of a slum.